A father figure…a dad.

That's how her son viewed him? He should've been more careful, not gotten so involved. Now he was leaving and the boy would be hurt.

"I'm sorry," he said.

"I never realized how much he missed having a man in his life. Not surprising, of course. In Jaye's eyes, you're a perfect image of what a father should be… strong, kind. Everything he longs for. Everything I didn't give him." She shook her head. "Maybe because I'm scared of letting someone in."

"You're not afraid of anything," he said, grasping her hand.

"I **am** afraid," she admitted, holding his glance. "I'm absolutely terrified. Of you. Of…this."

"Me, too," he said quietly.

"So what do we do?"

"I don't know. Ignore it. Go with it. Honestly, I have no idea." He rubbed her palm with his thumb. The action was hypnotic and sexy and she swayed toward him. He felt her heat. "I promised myself… I promised you that I'd keep my distance." He looked down at how close she was. "Ash, you should tell me to leave."

She touched his face, cradling his jaw. "I should…" she said, her words trailing. "But somehow, I can't."

The Cedar River Cowboys:
Riding into town with confidence on their own

THE RANCHER'S
UNEXPECTED
FAMILY

BY
HELEN LACEY

First Published in Great Britain 2017
By Mills & Boon, an imprint of HarperCollins*Publishers*
1 London Bridge Street, London, SE1 9GF

© 2017 Helen Lacey

ISBN: 978-0-263-92323-0

23-0817

Our policy is to use papers that are natural, renewable and recyclable products and made from wood grown in sustainable forests. The logging and manufacturing processes conform to the legal environmental regulations of the country of origin.

Printed and bound by
CPI Group (UK) Ltd, Croydon, CR0 4YY

Helen Lacey grew up reading *Black Beauty* and *Little House on the Prairie*. These childhood classics inspired her to write her first book when she was seven, a story about a girl and her horse. She loves writing for Mills & Boon Cherish, where she can create strong heroes with soft hearts and heroines with gumption who get their happily-ever-after. For more about Helen, visit her website, www.helenlacey.com.

For Nas Dean
Thank you for all that you do

Chapter One

There was one thing Cole Quartermaine knew, and that was that he knew *nothing* about how to handle surly teenagers.

In particular, *his* surly teenage daughter, who was sulking in the passenger seat of his rental car, earbuds plugged into her ears, her mouth pressed into a flat, grim line.

She hates me.

No surprise there. It had been a fraught eight months since he'd first discovered the existence of fourteen-year-old Maisy, and that he was father to a girl who had no interest in getting to know him or having any kind of relationship. But he desperately wanted to work things out with his daughter...no matter how much she resisted. She didn't care who he was, or that they shared the same blood. She called him Cole and he didn't insist she say anything different.

To be honest, he wasn't even sure how he'd react if she actually did call him *Dad*.

He concentrated on the drive and glanced to the right, at the sign welcoming them to town. Cedar River, South Dakota—population, three thousand and something. A speck on the map that sat in the shadow of the Black Hills. It was where he'd be staying for the next few weeks—a world away from Phoenix and the life he had there.

But he had to do it. For Maisy's sake. The last few months had been hard on them both. She didn't want to be with him, she didn't want anything to do with him or his folks or either of his younger sisters. And since the alternative was foster care, Cole knew this might be the only chance he had of truly connecting with his daughter. When his lawyer and friend, Joel, had suggested it, he'd resisted the idea. He wasn't a small-town kind of person. He had lived most of his life in Phoenix, Arizona, although he'd traveled the country extensively when he was competing on the NASCAR circuit. But now that he was retired from racing and managing his family-owned race team, Cole spent the majority of the year in his city apartment in Phoenix.

And this, he thought as he drove through Cedar River, with its one traffic light, wide wooden-planked sidewalks and mix of old and new storefronts, was not any kind of big city.

He checked the GPS and took a left turn, crossing the river over a long bridge that took them east, with another five miles to travel. When the electronic voice from the GPS told him they had arrived at their destination, Cole turned right and went through a pair of wide, whitewashed gates. He looked down the long gravel driveway and spotted a ranch house in the distance. There were several other buildings dotted around the house, most of them smaller except for the huge red barn with a white roof that stood out like a beacon beneath the glow of the midmorning sun. Several horses and about a dozen head of cattle were grazing in the pasture, and he spotted a couple of dogs roaming around the ranch house.

"We're here," he said, to himself more than anything, because his daughter hadn't spared him more than a surly glance for the last thirty miles.

Ignoring the heavy knot of tension in his gut, Cole pressed on the gas and headed down the driveway. He parked several yards from the main house and turned off the ignition, then unclipped his seat belt and turned toward his daughter.

"Maisy?" He waited for a reply.

After a moment she removed the earbuds and raised a bored eyebrow. "What?"

"We're here," he said again and nodded toward the windshield.

She glanced around and then shrugged. "Lucky me."

Cole fought the irritation climbing over his skin. He looked out the window and realized the place seemed deserted. Only the two large brown dogs were moving around the yard, circling the car warily. *Great*...maybe they were attack dogs. "Stay here," he instructed and grasped the door handle. "I'll be back in a minute."

She shrugged with a kind of disinterest he was becoming used to and popped the buds back into her ears. Cole looked at her and sighed as he got out of the car. One of the dogs barked as he closed the door and he took a couple of wary steps toward the house. He could hear music coming from the direction of the barn and then headed that way, watching as the dogs continued to circle around him as he walked. When he reached the barn he noticed how the hounds remained on either side of the door, as though they were standing on point and had been well trained to do so. The music was pure country and exactly what he'd expect to hear on a ranch on the outskirts of a town like Cedar River.

"Hello?" he said and walked through the wide doors.

He spotted an old truck in the corner, propped up on a set of jacks. Then he saw a pair of legs sticking out from beneath the tray, clad in jeans and attached to a set of curvy hips and then a bare, smooth belly peeking out of a grease-splattered T-shirt that was riding up over a taut set of abs. Cole came to an abrupt stop and stared at the shapely female form beneath the truck. His insides twitched with a kind instinctive reaction he suspected was wildly inappropriate, since he didn't have a clue who she was. But still, he let his gaze linger for a moment, before clearing his throat and saying hello again.

Then he heard a clang, a curse and then the hips shimmied across the ground and a woman sprang to her feet in front of him. The first things he noticed were her bright green eyes and thick red hair pulled back in a messy ponytail. His gaze traveled down her throat, her full breasts, her small waist and finally to her booted feet.

"Hey," she said loudly and clearly, so she could be heard above the music as she tugged down her T-shirt. "My face is up here!"

Heat smacked Cole squarely in his cheeks and he met her gaze instantly. She was younger than him, maybe around thirty, and was effortlessly pretty. There was a smear of grease on her forehead and another on her chin, but it did nothing to quell the instant and blisteringly hot attraction he experienced, like a bolt of lightning that came out of nowhere. Her green eyes glared at him and he bit back a grin. Feisty redheads weren't on his radar, not when he had more important things to worry about.

"My apologies," he said and kept his eyes locked with hers. "When I walked in here I didn't expect to find someone like you underneath the truck."

"Someone like me?" she queried, and regarded him as though he was a chauvinistic jerk who belonged in a cave. "Do you think women should stay in the kitchen and out of the garage?" she asked, and wiped her hands down her jeans, then turned off the radio.

"Not at all," Cole replied, his gaze unwavering. "I think it's helpful to be good at most things."

Her brows rose steeply. "And are you?"

"Good at most things?" He shrugged loosely. "Like most men I'd probably like to think so."

She laughed and the sound hit him directly in the middle of his chest. Then she held out her hand before he had a chance to speak. "You *must* be Mr. Quartermaine. I'm Ash McCune."

She's Ash McCune...

And not what he had been expecting. Joel had neglected to say how young *and* attractive his cousin was. Cole knew very little about her, other than the fact she was a police officer, a single mom and had been a foster mother to many kids during the past few years. Which is why he'd brought Maisy to her South Dakota ranch. He needed help with his daughter. And Joel had insisted that Ash McCune was exactly the lifeline he needed.

The moment their fingertips met, heat immediately shot up his arm. "Please, call me Cole."

"Sure," she said and removed her hand. "You're early. I wasn't expecting you until late this afternoon."

"Our flight was canceled and we had to switch to an earlier one. Is that a problem?"

She shrugged. "No problem. I just need some time to finish getting your cabin ready."

Awkwardness twitched between his shoulders. "I guess I should have called."

She shrugged again. "Like I said, no problem. I trust Joel explained our situation here?"

Cole's mouth twisted. "Actually, he was pretty vague about everything, other than the fact you graciously agree to allow Maisy and I to stay here for a few weeks."

"Maisy? That's your daughter?"

"Yes."

She nodded. "And she's fourteen?"

"She had a birthday last month," he replied.

"Does she know why she's here?"

Cole sighed. "She knows. And she's not happy about it."

Ash McCune's vibrant green eyes widened. "For the record, by the time they get here, most of the kids are re-sistant to the idea. And it usually works out."

"Usually?"

"Helping kids isn't an exact science," she explained. "And that's what we do here—we help kids." Her mouth twisted a little. "And the occasional parent."

His mouth twitched. "I'm glad to hear it. In my defense, I'm new to this parenting gig."

She nodded. "Joel told me. You've been friends with my cousin for a long time?"

"A few years. He dated my sister for a while a couple of years back. We've stayed friends and now he's my lawyer. Joel was convinced you'd be able to help Maisy."

"I'll do my very best," she said quietly. "But you do need to understand that I have no actual qualifications in child psychology. I'm an authorized foster-caregiver and have all the relevant documents to legally have children in my care. But there's nothing scientific about our methods. I guess what I'm trying to say is that we get results here through patience and kindness and caring."

"We?"

"My mom, Nancy, lives here and helps with the kids and I have an uncle who runs the ranching side of things."

He nodded fractionally. "You're a mother and a police officer, right?"

"Correct."

"Then I'd say you have all the qualifications you need."

She smiled and the action hit him way down low, in a place he'd somehow forgotten was there, and suddenly he felt about seventeen and keen to impress the cute girl in biology class. But he wasn't seventeen and this wasn't high school. It was real life. And he had a child who needed him to keep his head screwed on right.

"So… I should probably meet your daughter?"

Cole pulled himself from the foolish trance he was in and stepped back. "Of course. Ah, don't be surprised or offended if she's uncommunicative. My daughter doesn't say a lot."

"The sullen, silent type," she said and began walking from the barn. "I've handled that before."

And as he watched her hips sway as she walked from the barn, Cole was sure that Ash McCune could handle pretty much anything with one hand tied behind her back. Including him.

Good-looking men were nothing but trouble for a sensible, hardworking, small-town police officer and single mother. Logically, Ash knew that. But logic had spectacularly deserted her the moment she'd come face-to-face with Cole Quartermaine. Six foot something of lean, utterly gorgeous male with smooth brown skin, glittering blue eyes, broad shoulders and a sexy, megawatt smile wasn't what she'd been expecting.

I should have Googled him. Or at least asked Joel for more information.

Usually she knew more about the people whom she allowed to stay at her ranch. She knew he was rich and came from a prominent racing family in Phoenix. But when her cousin had assured her that Cole Quartermaine and his daughter were in dire need of her help, she'd agreed without resistance. She trusted Joel and all she'd been given were names, a brief and abridged history of Cole's occupation and the relationship between father and daughter, and an arrival date. She'd figured she'd simply find out anything else when they arrived.

Ergo, the hotter-than-Hades dad with the nice clothes and million-dollar smile who smelled absolutely *divine* was one major surprise.

And she didn't like surprises. Not ever.

As she strode from the barn she could feel his gaze burning through her. She straightened her back and kept walking, heading directly for the flashy new sedan parked in her driveway. The dogs were now beside her, doing their job. Milo and Mitzy were well trained and would restrain on command…but the only restraint needed in that moment was on her unexpectedly resurfacing libido!

Ash got to the rear of the car and waited. He walked around her and she got a waft of his aftershave…or soap, or shampoo, or maybe it was just her starved pheromones gone mad and she was imagining he smelled like a pine forest after the spring rain. Whatever it was, it struck her with the force of a freight train and she had to pull on every ounce of her usual good strength to not look like some kind of sex-starved idiot over a man she'd met just five minutes ago.

But boy, oh, boy…he was hot.

Ash watched as he tapped on the car window and then

waited as the door opened and a girl got out. She was extraordinarily beautiful, with dark curly hair, pale brown skin and blue eyes like her father's. She had a small piercing in her nose and several long chains dangling from her ears. But there was no smile, no indication she was even remotely pleased to be where she was.

"Hi," Ash said as cheerfully as she could muster and walked around the front of the vehicle. "I'm Ash McCune. And you're Maisy Quar—"

"Rayburn," the girl said stiffly. "Maisy Rayburn."

Ash saw Cole flinch slightly and made a mental note. Right. Relationship between father and daughter is exceptionally strained and she doesn't share his name.

"It's nice to meet you," Ash said and smiled. "I hope you'll enjoy your stay here."

The teenager's gaze darkened. "I'm here because *he* made me come," she said and jerked a thumb in her father's direction.

Ash glanced toward Cole. He was frowning and she felt her smile falter. He must have gotten her meaning because he quickly transformed the frown into a smile and when he did her insides immediately fluttered like a moth caught by the glow of a bulb. Damn…he was achingly gorgeous. Maybe the most delicious-looking man she had ever met. Perfectly put-together features, with just a touch of a whisker shadow and a military-style crew cut that amplified his good looks tenfold. Yep, Cole Quartermaine was obviously one of those men who had it all.

Great smile. *Check!*

Great shoulders. *Check!*

Great load of trouble ahead. *Check!*

"How about we head inside for some iced tea?" she suggested.

"I'd rather just go to my room," the teenager said.

"I have to finish getting the cabin ready," Ash said and pointed to a small building about one hundred feet from the ranch house. "And we should probably get to know one another first."

The young girl's expression narrowed instantly. "We're staying in there? Are you kidding me? What a dump."

"Maisy!"

Cole's voice was sharply disapproving and his daughter recoiled for a second before shrugging her shoulders in a willful way that spoke volumes. Ash did her best not to take offense. She'd been a cop for over a decade and had fostered nearly twenty-five children during that time, so a thick and resilient skin was a necessity. But there was no doubt the man standing by the car was not as adept at handling teenage stubbornness and anger. Compassion for him quickly coursed through her blood, along with a deep-rooted and heartfelt ache for the girl who looked so solitary and mad at the world.

"The cabin is clean and tidy," Ash said and walked toward the porch. When she mounted the first step she turned on her heels. "Things aren't always what they seem. Take me, for instance," she said, shoulders back as she met Maisy's glare head-on. "Five feet four and one hundred and twenty-five pounds wringing wet—some people might think I'm a pushover. Those people would be wrong. Come inside the house, you can take your bags up to the cabin later."

Ash turned and walked up to the house, opening the door and screen. She waited for her guests to follow and then stood back as they crossed the threshold. Cole ushered his daughter up the steps and Ash managed a tight smile as they moved through the doorway. She closed the screen and walked down the hallway, over the shiny polished floors and into the large kitchen at the rear of the

house. The warmth of red cedar cupboards and dark gran-
ite countertops struck her as it always did. She'd had the
kitchen renovated a year earlier and loved spending time
in the big room, with its large scrubbed table and chairs
and the pots hanging above the stove. Ash loved to cook
and did so whenever she could shoo her mother out from
behind the counter. Fifty-seven-year-old Nancy Olsen-
McCune-Rodriguez was twice-married, twice-divorced
and Ash's right hand on the ranch. Along with Uncle Ted,
her mother's much older brother, who was essentially the
ranch foreman and lived in one of the four cabins behind
the main house. And of course, Jaye, her twelve-year-old
son, whom she loved more than anything.

She washed and dried her hands and ignored the fact
her clothes were grease-stained and she probably looked
like an oily rag. "So, iced tea?" she asked and looked at her
two guests, who were hovering in the doorway.

"Sure," Cole said and stepped farther into the room.
"Nice place you've got here."

Ash nodded. "My grandparents bought the ranch over
fifty years ago. When they died they left it to my uncle
and Mom and me," she said and grabbed the jug of iced
tea from the refrigerator, then filled up three glasses with
ice and a sprig of mint. "We run a few head of cattle and
some horses. And we have chickens, an adorable alpaca
and a few goats."

"And two big dogs."

She met his gaze and smiled a little. "They look formi-
dable, but they're quite civilized."

"*He* hates dogs."

Maisy's voice was muffled but decipherable and Ash
raised a brow. "More of a cat person, are you?"

He shrugged. "Not especially," he replied and glanced

toward his daughter. "And I don't hate dogs. I just have… allergies," he said and shrugged again.

"*He's* allergic to everything." Maisy again, even more disagreeable than before.

Ash's eyes widened. "Everything?"

She noticed his cheeks darken. "Not everything. Bees," he explained. "And shellfish."

"Then I shall try not to poison you with my seafood paella," Ash said and smiled. "I trust you have an EpiPen on standby?"

"Always."

"My son has a nut allergy, so I'm well-rehearsed in emergency trips to the ER."

"Let's hope it doesn't come to that," he said and his mouth twitched in a half smile that sent her awareness of him skyrocketing. "As long as I stay out of your flower bed and avoid your paella, I'm sure I'll be fine."

Flirting…

For one crazy moment that's what it felt like. Which was ridiculous, since his daughter was standing in the room and Ash hadn't known him for more than fifteen minutes. But still, the notion lingered. Ash filled up the glasses and passed them around, careful not to get too close to the man now sitting on the far side of the dining table. She pushed the glass across the table and invited Maisy to take a seat. The teenager shrugged, clearly feigning an overinterest in the music coming from the buds she had in her ears so she wouldn't have to talk. Ash was familiar with the ploy and pulled out a chair for Maisy, opposite her father.

"Take a seat," she said and smiled.

The girl cranked her gaze toward her for a moment, then plunked heavily in the seat. "Sure. Whatever."

Ash moved around the table and sat down, then directed

her gaze straight onto the angry-looking teenage at the end of the table. "So, Maisy, tell me why you're here?"

Dark blue eyes flicked up and glared at her. "Because *he* made me."

"Yes, so you said," Ash said with controlled patience. "I want to know why *you* think you're here."

She shrugged. "So I get to stay out of social services."

"Is that where you think you were heading?"

"Ask *him*," she said and jerked her thumb once again in her father's direction. "He's got all the answers."

Hot Dad was about to respond when Ash held up a hand. "I'm asking you, Maisy."

The teenager shrugged again, but wouldn't look at her. "I dunno...maybe. I've done some stuff."

"Stuff?"

Maisy glanced up, her gaze angry and resentful. "I stole a stupid book from a stupid store and got busted. They called the cops and then *he* had to bail me out."

Ash took a sip of tea and nodded. "Do you like to read?"

The teen's expression narrowed suspiciously. "Read? Yeah, I guess."

"We have quite an extensive bookshelf here," Ash said and smiled. "In the front living room. My mother is an avid reader and collects all kind of books. You're welcome to read as many as you like while you're here. Or there's a great library in town, if you prefer."

"I like fantasy books."

"So does my mom," Ash said quietly. "She's going to enjoy having someone to talk to about them. I'm not much of a reader, unless it's a cookbook."

Maisy unexpectedly rattled off the names of several of her favorite authors and titles before settling her gaze back into her lap and then clearly upping the music volume. But Ash was pleased with their exchange. Small steps, she knew, were hard at first, but well worth the effort when it came to a lost child.

Now all she had to do was get Cole Quartermaine out of the hot-dad category and everything would be fine.

Yep…easy.

Not.

Cole couldn't believe what he was witnessing. Maisy communicating. Maisy talking. Maisy actually connecting with someone. In that moment he could have gotten up and kissed Ash McCune for getting his usually uncommunicative daughter to have something that actually resembled a real conversation.

Kiss Ash McCune…

Okay, maybe not.

For one, she looked feisty enough to hit him over the head with a frying pan. And secondly, thinking about kissing her was plain old stupid. Despite the fact he found her so attractive. He was in Cedar River for one thing—his daughter. Nothing was going to derail that. Not the fact that he'd suddenly discovered he had a thing for redheads.

"My mother homeschools, by the way," Ash said, getting his attention. "Four hours every weekday. In case you were concerned about Maisy keeping up with her schoolwork."

He nodded. "How many kids do you have staying here right now?"

"Three," she replied and glanced toward his daughter and then back to him. "Four. Plus one."

He didn't think he'd ever been anyone's *plus one* before. Cole kept his gaze locked with hers and heat instantly climbed over his limbs. He ignored the feeling and drank some tea, which tasted like poison and made him grimace.

"Not a tea drinker I take it?"

He shrugged loosely. "More a coffee and beer kind of guy."

Her expression narrowed fractionally. "This is a dry ranch with a strict no-alcohol rule."

Great. "Sure."

"For the kids' benefit," she explained. "Troubled teens and alcohol can be a bad mix. So, I keep the place free of the stuff. Much to the dismay of my uncle Ted."

Cole understood. "I'm not much of a drinker," he said quietly and endured another sip of the poisonous beverage in front of him.

"We also have a no-smoking rule."

He looked up and met her green gaze. "I haven't lit a cigarette since I was twenty-one."

She sipped her tea and smiled. "Sounds like you are vice-free."

Cole's skin prickled. "I'm as flawed as anyone else."

Her eyes widened for a moment and it was incredibly sexy. Even the grease mark still on her chin was sexy. He wondered why every word between them sounded like some kind of crazy flirtation. He wasn't in the market for flirting. For anything. And definitely not with a woman like Ash McCune. He didn't do relationships anymore. He kept his love life casual and had since he'd split with his ex-wife and gotten out of their two-year marriage a few years earlier—he'd lost his house, his heart and a good chunk of his savings.

Cole shrugged off the memory and got to his feet. "We should probably unpack."

She stared at him for a moment. "Sure. I'll just get the bed linen. I'll meet you outside."

He took off as though his heels were on fire, instructing Maisy to follow. By the time he was at the car and had taken their luggage from the trunk, the knot of tension in his shoulders had lessened. Until Ash McCune came around the porch and down the steps, carrying a wicker laundry basket piled with sheets and towels.

She swayed when she walked. *Swayed.* Damn.

Get a grip, Quartermaine.

Cole grabbed both his and Maisy's suitcases and left his daughter to bring his laptop and her small tote. He stayed several feet back as he followed Ash around the rear of the house and toward the largest of the five cabins that were all within a couple of hundred yards of the main house. She placed the basket on one hip, climbed the steps, opened the door and then walked inside. Cole did the same, instructing Maisy to follow, but her cell rang and his daughter quickly dropped her bag onto the porch near the door and sat down on the step. Figuring it was one of her school friends, he told her not to take too long and gave her some privacy, then entered the house.

The cabin was roomy and open plan, with raked ceilings, a small kitchen and dining area and a large living space. There were a couple of mismatched sofas, a cabinet that housed a television, a gaming console and a large stone fireplace and hearth. It looked clean and comfortable and very livable.

"There are two bedrooms," she explained. "The fridge and pantry are stocked with the basics, but if you have any special dietary requirements, there's a supermarket in town. You're also welcome to join us for dinner at the main house whenever you like."

Cole nodded and followed her down the short hallway. She walked into a room on her left and placed the basket on the double bed. There was a robe, a small dresser and a chair in the corner and a worn rug on the floor. Cole thought about his huge penthouse apartment, with its modern decor and city views. He'd bought the place after his divorce, fully furnished and without any mementos from his failed marriage.

"I'm sure we'll be comfortable, thank you."

"Would you like me to make the bed up?" she asked.

He realized they were standing on opposite sides of the bed and met her gaze head-on. He glanced at the mattress and the serviceable blue patterned quilt draped over the bottom frame. "I've been making my own bed since I was eight years old, so I'm pretty sure I can manage."

One of her incredibly sexy eyebrows arched dramatically. "Well, you did say you were good at most things."

Cole's pulse quickened and he motioned toward the bed between them. Awareness flared up, fanned by how the small room suddenly seemed absurdly intimate. "Would you like me to prove it?"

Her mouth opened slightly and she gasped. "Huh?"

Cole didn't miss the startled look in her eyes. "We could…" He paused, fascinated as color rose up her neck, hueing her pale skin. Without even knowing how it happened, there was enough heat combusting the air between them to start a fire. "We could make it together. The bed, I mean."

She swallowed hard and stepped back. "I don't think… I'm sure you'll manage without me."

Cole smiled and half shrugged. "Of course. But it won't be anywhere near as much fun."

The innuendo was obvious and she turned beet red. And then fled.

It was, he realized, still smiling to himself as he watched her retreating figure disappear through the doorway, going to be a very long three weeks.

Chapter Two

I am officially the most foolish woman on the planet.

Ash was still cussing herself twenty minutes later as she washed up and changed into fresh jeans and a red blouse. Then she opened her laptop and typed in the name *Cole Quartermaine.*

She clicked several of the links that came up, scanned the pages and sat back on the bed, looking at the images on the screen. The Quartermaines were an old-money family in Phoenix. His third-generation Irish Catholic father had a mop of auburn hair and sparkling blue eyes, and his African American mother was so beautiful she looked like a movie star. He had two sisters, both younger. One was a lawyer, the other a marketing executive who worked in the family business. Cole had been born into a NAS-CAR empire and had a promising career as a driver until a near-fatal accident when he was twenty-seven. Now he managed the family's team alongside his father. It was impressive stuff.

There were several pictures of him with an array of beautiful women and she figured a man who looked like Cole didn't have to work hard to get female company. She'd read that he had an ex-wife and there was no mention of a current significant other.

By the time she returned to the kitchen it was past two o'clock. Her mother and uncle would be home later that afternoon, along with Jaye and the three kids currently staying at the ranch. They'd headed into town that morning for haircuts and lunch at JoJo's Pizza Parlor and to give Ash some much needed time to do a few repairs on the old truck that had seen better days. But she wasn't in the mood to spend any more time under the hood. She planned on making a roast for dinner that night, so set about preparing the meal and getting the meat into the oven. Then she pulled one of her mother's signature peach pies out of the freezer and left it to thaw on the counter.

From the kitchen window she had a clear view of all the cabins and wandered back and forth a few times to see if there was any movement from the one now occupied by her newest guests. But nothing. She made a pot of coffee and looked through the pantry for something to snack on, settling on a half-eaten packet of rice crackers.

Note to self—must stop thinking about a certain hot dad. Focus on the real reason he's here.

Easy.

Ash was dipping into the packet for her third cracker when there was a knock on the door of the back mudroom, which was just off the kitchen. She turned on her heels. The door was open and Cole stood there, looking so totally gorgeous as he rested one strong shoulder against the jamb that her mouth turned dry and the cracker she was eating suddenly felt like sandpaper as it lodged in her throat.

"Oh...hello," she said and coughed, then coughed again, quickly making her way around the counter for some water. She poured a glass, still coughing. She took a few sips, but the itching in her throat remained and she coughed again. And again. Until her eyes starting watering and she had to bend over to alleviate the dry, choking sensation.

Then she felt an unexpected hand on her back. A large, soothing hand that patted her gently between the shoulder blades. The coughing quickly subsided and she swallowed hard, feeling the heat of his touch through the cotton shirt she wore. Ash straightened immediately, swiveling on her heels. Which only heightened the intimacy of the space between them—which was no space at all. His hand remained on her back and they were close enough that she could see he had a small scar on his temple and another under his chin. And the scent of him once again assailed her senses. Never in her life had she been so intensely aware of a man—particularly one she'd known less than an hour. But this man made her remember that she was more than a mom, a rancher and a police officer...and that she was very much a flesh-and-blood woman.

"Are you okay now?" he asked quietly, dropping his hand.

Ash stepped back and nodded. "Ah, yes... I'm fine."

"I'm sorry if I startled you," he said and moved around the counter.

"Oh, no problem, I feel fine now. What can I do for you?"

"I thought we should talk," he said and met her gaze. "About Maisy. You probably have some questions and I'd like to discuss this without my daughter in earshot."

"That's a good idea," Ash said, regaining her equilibrium and good sense as she poured coffee into two mugs, and then asked the first obvious question. "Can you tell me about her mother?"

He shrugged a little uncomfortably. "Her name was Deanna. She died eight months ago. Pancreatic cancer."

"I'm so sorry," Ash said, handing him one of the mugs.

"Don't be," he said quickly and then frowned when he realized how odd his reply must have sounded. "I mean, of course, yes, it's tragic for someone so young…and for Maisy. But I didn't know her very well."

Ash's brow came up instantly. "Really?"

"Well, of course I knew her," he said, clearly uncomfortable. "You want the story, here it is—nearly fifteen years ago I knew her for three days. I was twenty-two, she was twenty. We met at a race and we hooked up, spending three nights together. I never saw her again after that. And then eight months ago a woman from social services knocked on my door and told me I had a teenage daughter."

She sat down opposite him. "Deanna never let you know she was pregnant?"

He shook his head. "It wasn't exactly a love match. It was a weekend."

"How do you think you would have reacted had she told you from the beginning?"

He shrugged again. "I'm not sure. At the time my life was hectic. I'd just won my first major race and I was regularly traveling around the country. And I wasn't interested in anything serious. But I'd like to believe I would have tried to do the right thing. I'll never know. All I know is that now I *am* in a position to do what's right…and that's to try and have some kind of relationship with my daughter and give her a home."

Ash admired his honesty. "She seems very resistant to the idea."

"She hates my guts," he said bluntly. "But I'm all she's got."

"Are there any relatives on her mother's side?"

"None," he replied. "Her parents have both passed away and there are only a couple of very distant cousins in Wichita. My parents and both my sisters have tried to help, even offering to have Maisy go and live with them."

"But?" Ash prompted.

"She says she doesn't want that, either. Frankly, I'm all out of ideas."

Ash nodded. "But you want her to be with you?"

"Of course," he snapped back quickly. "She's my kid. I'm her father. We're family. And family is everything. I just need to work out how to get her to at least *like* me."

"She doesn't have to like you," Ash said earnestly. "She doesn't have to love you. You just have to love her. No one tells you that when you become a parent—it's something we all learn in our own time and our own way. She'll come around, but you need to be prepared for a lot of difficulty in between. Anger, despair and probably a lot of silence. As irrational as it seems, she probably blames you for her mother's death."

His blue eyes glittered. "You're right."

"And telling her that you didn't know about her up until eight months ago will make no difference to her adolescent logic."

"You're right again. You can figure that out by one short conversation with her? How?"

Ash drank her coffee and then cradled the mug between her hands. "Experience. She needs someone to blame for her unhappiness and you're it. You'll need a thick skin to get through the next few weeks."

His mouth creased in a half smile. "My mom is black, my dad is white and I grew up in a city that is predominantly white and Hispanic. A thick skin was a necessary part of growing up."

Ash nodded slightly. "I guess we all have our trials. I was reading a few articles about you earlier," she said and drank some coffee.

"Really?"

"I Googled," she explained. "Mostly about your career and the family business."

He shrugged lightly. "The family *dynasty*," he said. "Three generations of grease monkeys. My grandfather made sure all the grandsons learned our trade under the hood before we were allowed behind the wheel."

"Not the granddaughters?" she inquired.

"We're an equal-opportunity family," he said and grinned. "However, both my sisters preferred college to the garage and our five cousins are all male. But you never know, Maisy might just decide to pick up a wrench instead of a textbook."

Ash raised a brow. "Good answer. If that's the case, I may get you to take a look at my old truck. The brake line needs replacing and the darn thing keeps overheating."

"No problem," he replied. "I'd like to earn my keep while we're here, since Joel made it very clear that you refuse to take any kind of financial assistance from me."

"You'll only be here a few weeks," she reminded him. "That won't make me broke."

He sighed. "I'd still like to pay my way."

She shook her head. "I'm doing this as a favor for Joel. And because I want to help you."

"I appreciate that, but –"

"Money muddies the waters," she said, interrupting him and then she chewed on her bottom lip.

"Maybe," he said and looked at her mouth for a second. "I've never really had to worry about it."

"Lucky you," she said wryly. "I shall make sure I stir your coffee with a silver spoon from now on."

He laughed and the sound made her heart beat faster.

When he spoke again she was barely able to meet his gaze. "I guess that comment did make me sound like a pompous ass. Which I assure you, I'm not. My grandfather didn't believe in free rides in life, and my dad feels the same."

"Sounds like you've had strong role models," she remarked. "That will be good for Maisy. Tell me about your mother—I saw a picture when I was surfing the web. She's striking."

"She's the best," he replied quickly. "And she's tried to develop a relationship with my daughter in the last few months, but Maisy…" He shrugged. "Small steps, I guess."

Ash nodded. "Absolutely. Once Maisy works out that you're not her enemy, I'm sure she'll take comfort in the rest of your family, too. Thank you for being candid."

"We're living at your home, imposing on your generosity, so I have no intention of whitewashing how bad things have become."

Ash's insides contracted. He genuinely cared for his daughter and she felt a sudden surge of compassion for him. "Has it been difficult from the beginning?"

"She's been in trouble pretty much since she came to live with me," he replied. "Once it was confirmed that she was my daughter I sought full custody. Since there were no other close relatives it was granted and she moved into my apartment. But it was hard. Maisy didn't want to be there. Actually, I'm sure she didn't know what she wanted. But I enrolled her in school and then within a couple of weeks I got a call from the principal about truancy and smoking.

She was suspended for a week and then we had the issue with the shoplifting and she got hauled down to the police station. Thankfully, Joel got the charges dropped, but I knew she was getting deeper into trouble. And frankly, I was all out of options until your cousin suggested we come here."

"Can I offer some advice?"

He nodded. "That's what I was hoping for."

"Don't expect too much, too soon," she said and sighed. "She's obviously still grieving for her mom and learning to trust you will take time. You need to put aside any impatience or judgment and simply let her...*be*. Tell me, does she have a boyfriend?"

His eyes rolled. "God, I hope not."

Ash chuckled. "Well, she's fourteen, and fourteen-year-old girls think about all that."

"It's what fourteen-year-old boys think about that worries me."

She met his gaze. It was steady. Unwavering. She suspected he was always like that. Strong. Reliable. He'd clearly embraced the responsibility of his child, which said plenty about his measure. Ash admired that. Some people didn't have the backbone for that kind of responsibility.

Like Pete.

A little voice reminded her that now was not the time to reminisce about Pete Shapiro and his many failings. She knew them as though they were carved within the very fiber of her soul.

"Well, there are no fourteen-year-old boys here at the moment, so you can relax."

He sat back and the chair creaked. "You said you had three kids here right now?"

She nodded. "Yes. Tahlia, she's eight. Her brother, Micah, is nine. And Ricky is seventeen."

His brows came together. "Seventeen?"

Ash smiled. "No need to worry, he's not interested in girls. At all," she added. "Which is part of the reason why he's here. His parents can't accept that he's gay and it's been a tough time for him."

He nodded. "I look forward to meeting them. And your son, of course."

Ash's heart warmed. "Jaye is amazing. He's my whole world."

"Can I ask about his father?"

"You can ask," she replied. "He's not on the scene and hasn't been for a long time. And I'd prefer the subject not to come up around my son."

"Sure," he said easily. "Anything else off-limits? Old boyfriend? Current boyfriend?"

"No boyfriend," she responded.

"Have the men in this town all got blindfolds on?"

Even if it wasn't meant that way, his words sounded pretty flirtatious, and they both knew it. Heat, bright and damning, rose up her neck and throat and smacked her directly in the cheeks like a cattle brand. She got to her feet and pushed in the chair. Coffee was over. She had chores to do. And blue eyes to escape from.

"You should come for dinner tonight," she said quietly. "That way you and Maisy can meet everyone. So, about six?"

He stood and nodded, obviously aware he was being dismissed. "Thank you. See you later."

For a time after he left, Ash still smelled the traces of his cologne in the air. It was nice, sort of woodsy and masculine, and it did a whole bunch of things to her usual good sense. She shook the notion off and started packing the dishwasher and once the dishes were done, Ash picked up her phone and called her friend Nicola Radici. She wanted to vent and Nicola was exactly the ear she needed.

"So, he's hot and single?" Nicola asked after Ash told her friend about her new guests, including how unfairly attractive Cole was. "How awful for you."

Ash bit back a grin. "Yes. Inconveniently so."

"Are you looking for sympathy?" Nicola queried and laughed.

Ash was about to respond when her son came through the door. Her heart flipped over at the sight of him. He was the light of her life. She ended the call, telling Nicola they would catch up soon, and then gave her son her full attention, briefly answering his questions about the new arrivals, and then she made him a snack. It gave her something to do and took her mind off things.

And off a certain, six-foot-something, utterly gorgeous man she suspected was destined to invade her thoughts and dreams for the foreseeable future.

When Cole returned to the cabin Maisy was sitting on one of the sofas, feet curled lotus-style, head down as she looked at her cellphone.

"Everything okay?" he asked when he spotted her.

"The cell reception here sucks," she complained and held her phone above her shoulder with a dramatic scowl.

"It might be better outside," he suggested. "We can go for a walk and look around if you like."

She shrugged and stood. "I'm gonna go to my room."

Cole watched her retreat down the hall and then heard a door slam. Every conversation was a battle. Every look one of defiance. Every interaction filled with rage. She was lost. Out of reach. And he had no idea how to connect with her.

He dropped into the sofa, defeated, wondering if coming to the ranch had been a good idea. At the time Joel had suggested it, Cole felt as though he'd been given a lifeline. But now, he wasn't so sure. It was just geography. Maisy was still Maisy. He was still the one person she seemed to hate above everyone else.

She's doesn't have to love you. You just have to love her.

Ash's words scrambled around in his head. She was right. But he still didn't know how he should feel about them. The moment he'd discovered he had a daughter, he'd made every effort to do the right thing. It had been a no-brainer to have the required DNA test and then go to court to get custody. As scared as he was about the idea of being a father, she was his daughter, his *blood*. His parents had been over the moon at the idea of being grandparents and his sisters had immediately embraced Maisy into the family. It was Maisy who dragged her feet. Of course he understood—her mother was dead and she felt alone. But she wasn't, and that was the most damnable and frustrating thing. He *wanted* to be her father, if she would just meet him halfway.

He stretched out and closed his eyes as fatigue settled into his muscles. It had been a long few days. Firstly, getting Maisy to agree to come to South Dakota had been challenging, especially when she insisted she was happy to go into the foster-care system. But he didn't believe her. Sometimes, he was sure he saw glimpses of her actually settling into the life they had together, but her resistance was like a wall she felt she needed to keep up. One he wasn't sure he could ever break down.

Cole sighed and relaxed against the scratchy sofa. It would work out. He had to believe that. He dozed for a while and when he awoke it was after five o'clock. Maisy was in her room and he tapped on her door and told her they were going up to the main house at six for dinner. He headed to his own room to unpack, and then shower and change. When he returned to the living room Maisy was standing by the fireplace, earbuds in their usual position.

"Ready to go?" he asked.

She shrugged. "Do I have a choice, Cole?"

The way she used his name made his nerves twitch. "No."

Her scowl increased. "Then I guess I'm ready."

They left the cabin and walked up to the house, side by side. Maisy's arms were tightly crossed and he suspected he was in for one of her dark moods. He'd tried to get her to open up about her mom, but she'd always responded with some snappy retort about how he didn't know anything about her and it didn't matter since her mom was dead. And guilt always seemed to manifest itself in him whenever she talked about her mother. For Cole, Deanna was a dim memory. A pretty, young blonde woman he barely recalled. There'd been a lot of women back then. A lot of beds. A lot of meaningless sex and awkward morning-afters. That changed after the accident that almost killed him when he was twenty-seven. He'd spent three weeks in a coma, with a broken back, busted left arm, smashed-up kneecap and so many cuts and bruises he looked like he'd gone through a meat grinder. Four months in hospital, several surgeries and six months of rehab had taught him not to take anything for granted. The accident ended his racing career and drafted him into an early retirement from the track. Now, he managed the team and crew, including his cousin Lance, who was regularly one of the top three drivers in the country at the end of each season. He missed racing, but his cobbled-together bones weren't able to withstand the endless workout that the NASCAR circuit demanded. And since he'd done everything he could to make sure he didn't spend his life in a wheelchair, he wasn't about to do anything that risked his long-term health. Even though the sidelines weren't as glamourous, didn't have the adrenaline rush of a podium finish, he could at least live the rest of his life on his feet.

Then he'd met Valerie. Beautiful, smart, self-destructive Valerie. He'd loved her. Married her. Divorced her. And then done his best to forget her.

Cole shook off the memory and walked around the front of the house. He could hear laughter and the sound of clinking crockery. It sounded a whole lot like dinner at his parents' house and the idea made him smile. He climbed the steps, waited for Maisy to catch up and then tapped on the front screen door.

A woman around sixty, dressed in moleskins and a glittery chambray shirt and boots, appeared behind the screen and gave him a beaming smile. "Well, hello, there. I'm Nancy, Ash's mother. Please come in."

Cole introduced himself and Maisy as they were ushered down the hall and into a large dining room. The table in the center of the room was wide and covered in a tablecloth, while dinnerware and an array of platters ran down the center. Dinner was clearly a big deal on the McCune ranch.

There were several other people present—an older man he assumed was her uncle and three kids, a boy and a girl who were clearly siblings of Native American heritage, and a teenage boy with heavily gelled and spiked black hair. He also sported a couple of piercings in his top lip and a dragon tattoo on his neck. Cole wasn't one to judge, since he'd gone through his own ink stage as a youngster. The older boy, Ricky, shook his hand and then grunted in a friendly sort of way in Maisy's direction. Ash's uncle came around the table to shake his hand and once the introductions were done, Nancy said she was heading to the kitchen for a round of drinks.

"Wish it was beer," Uncle Ted said quietly so that only Cole could hear and grinned.

Another child appeared in the doorway. He had a shock of curly red hair and a face load of freckles. He also had a brace on his left leg and used a cane.

"Hi, I'm Jaye," he said and ambled slowly toward them, a noticeable hitch in his gait.

Cole didn't miss the disinterest in Maisy's expression. "It's good to meet you, Jaye," Cole said, and introduced Maisy, who gave a half-hearted wave. "I've heard a lot about you."

"I've heard a lot about you, too," the kid said cheerfully. "My mom was talking about you on the phone to someone today," he said and then frowned a little and shrugged. "Though I probably wasn't meant to hear it. Or tell you."

Cole laughed softly. He already liked the boy. "Well, it'll be our secret, okay?"

Jaye's freckled face beamed. "Sure thing. Mom doesn't ever need to know."

"Mom doesn't ever need to know what?"

Cole's gaze instantly shifted to the doorway. Silhouetted in the door frame and wearing a short green dress that shimmied around her thighs and showed off a truly sensational pair of legs, Ash McCune just about dropped him to his knees. He noticed her hair was out of its band and fell just past her shoulders. Cole stared and then swallowed hard, trying to get his wayward thoughts off her smooth calves and the curves that had somehow managed to consume his thoughts for most of the afternoon.

I'm in big trouble.

"Nothing, Mom," Jaye said and grinned. "Just guy stuff."

She smiled and Cole's stomach took a dive. Damn, she was beautiful.

"So you've met everyone?" she asked as she came into the room and stood behind her son, dropping her hands onto his shoulders.

"Yes."

"Mom said you used to be a race car driver," Jaye said, beaming up at him.

"That's right."

The boy's bright green eyes widened. "I'd *love* to drive a race car. That would be so cool. Mom said that maybe next year I can enter the soapbox-derby races at the spring fair. I'd like to enter this year though," he said and shrugged. "I've already got a plan drawn up for my cart and—"

"I said next year...*maybe*," Ash said and kissed the top of his head. "Now, how about you show Mr. Quartermaine and Maisy to their seats and we can all eat?" she said to the whole room.

A minute later they were all seated and Nancy had returned with a pitcher of homemade lemonade that she placed in the center of the table. Uncle Ted said a short prayer before they ate and everyone stayed quiet, including Maisy. Cole had been raised in a strict Catholic household, but rarely went to church except for weddings and funerals. He found himself seated between Maisy and Uncle Ted, and while his daughter was sullen and uncommunicative during the entire meal, the older man talked incessantly about everything from motor racing to the current price of barley and wheat, and the last time he'd visited the nearby Mount Rushmore. Cole didn't mind, though. Ted was friendly and personable, telling funny stories about the ranch and his years in the navy. But Cole was distracted. With Ash only a couple of seats away and holding court with the kids, who chatted about their day out, their haircuts and the upcoming spring fair, he couldn't help but be aware of her as she laughed and bantered with her son and the two youngest children. There was a kind of natural energy around her, and he realized how out of the loop he'd been lately when it came to being around an attractive woman. He hadn't been on a date for six months. And hadn't had sex in longer than that.

Almost as though on cue, he met her gaze across the table. She was smiling just a little, as though she had some great secret only she was privy to. He wanted to look away, but couldn't. Her smile deepened and he watched as she blushed. Whatever was going on, Cole's instincts told him she was feeling it, too. He gave himself a mental shake, turned his attention back to his food and tried to start a conversation with his daughter, who'd barely spoken a word since they'd sat down for dinner. He managed to get a few sentences out of her and by the time the plates were cleared she was talking quietly to Ricky about music and the latest boy band. He relaxed a bit and pushed back the chair, got up and grabbed a few of the dishes still left on the table. The younger kids and Ted had moved into the adjoining living room to watch television and Cole headed for the kitchen.

Ash was alone, loading the dishwasher, but she stopped the task when she noticed the plates in his hands. "Oh, thanks so much."

"No problem," he said and placed them on the counter. "You're an amazing cook."

Her mouth curved. "Thank you. But the peach pie was my mom's doing. Some secret recipe she's been threatening to share for years, but still hasn't. Can you cook?"

"Not a lick," he replied and grinned. "Spoiled, silver spoon, only son—you get the picture."

She laughed. "Can you make coffee?"

He nodded. "Sure."

She waved an arm in the direction of the coffeepot. "Then you're on beverage duty while I keep stacking."

Cole moved around the counter. "You're bossy, anyone ever tell you that?"

She laughed again. "Of course. Just ask my son and Uncle Ted."

He grabbed the coffeepot. "He's a great kid, by the way."

"I know," she said quietly. "And you can ask, if you want."

Cole rested his behind on the countertop. "Ask?"

"About Jaye," she explained. "And his condition. He had an accident when he was two and half years old and was badly injured. There were surgeries and—and he…"

"He's a great kid," Cole said again when her words trailed off. "That's all I see."

She stopped what she was doing and turned, resting her hip against the counter, arms crossed loosely. "Thank you."

"For what?"

"For not looking at me with the kind of pitying expression I usually get from parents of able-bodied children."

"I don't pity you," he said. "Or Jaye. He's obviously bright and well-adjusted."

"Yes. And he loves reading and music and art."

"And soapbox-derby racing?" he said, one brow raised. "He mentioned several times that he wants to enter this year."

She nodded. "I know. Maybe next year. I may be an overprotective parent, but I don't want him to get hurt, either physically or emotionally. The races can be really competitive and some of the other kids and their parents take it so seriously. I don't want him to be singled out or be disadvantaged because of his disability."

"That's a fair call," he said and rested his hands on the edge of the countertop. "But I don't imagine you can protect him from soapbox spills or schoolyard bullies twenty-four seven."

"My son is homeschooled," she said pointedly. "And you're right, I can't watch him every minute of every day. But while he's still a child, while he's here under this roof, I'm sure as heck gonna try."

Cole grinned. She had a lot of spunk. He liked it. He liked her. And it was getting more intense the more time he spent with her. Something had to give. One of them had to say what was now glaringly obvious.

He turned so they were facing one another. The heat between them had ramped up another notch. And then another. "Can I say something that might be highly inappropriate?"

She met his gaze without blinking. "Go ahead."

He took a breath. "I'm…the thing is… Even though I know it's kind of crazy because we've only just met, I'm really… I'm really attracted to you."

The air between them was suddenly thick with silence and he immediately expected outrage. But it didn't come. Instead, she inhaled deeply and spoke. "I know. It's mutual."

"But it's out of the question, right?"

She nodded. "Absolutely."

"And if I forget that over the course of the next few weeks, will you smack me upside the head to bring me to my senses?"

"If that's what you want."

"I think we both know," he said quietly, "what I want. This is about what's best. I need to keep my head screwed on straight while I'm here, for Maisy's sake."

"I agree."

She was in agreement. It was all going to work out fine. But still, Cole wasn't entirely convinced that they could ignore the tension and awareness between them.

He pushed himself off the counter. "Great," he said as he passed her and headed for the door. When he reached the doorway, he turned. "I think I'll skip the coffee. And, Ash," he said, looking into her eyes. "Maybe you shouldn't wear that sexy little dress anymore. Because it seriously messes with my good intentions."

Chapter Three

He thought she was sexy.

Ash turned hot all over just thinking about it. Had she ever considered herself sexy before? Probably not. It made her feel like someone else. Someone she didn't know.

She wasn't that person. She was the person other people confided in. In high school she was the girl always put into the friends-only category. Even her relationship with Pete had started out in the friendship zone. They'd been lab partners and then study buddies and then one night, over hot dogs and Kool-Aid, he'd kissed her clumsily. They dated for the last two years of high school and by then she knew they were perfect for one another. They'd talked about their future, made plans and imagined their wedding day and everything that would follow. She would join the police department while he would become an apprentice mechanic at a garage in town. Then they would travel and see the world together and one day start a family and live happily ever after. But then she got pregnant a year out of high school and everything changed. Not at first. In the beginning, Pete seemed as happy as she was. They got engaged and agreed they'd marry once the baby came. Jaye was born—beautiful and precious. But soon, her dreams turned to dust. Pete wasn't interested in being a father. He was more interested in his motorcycle and drinking and other women.

The wedding was postponed and their relationship deteriorated. After Jaye's accident things got worse because Pete had been watching him that afternoon. Or not watching him, as it had turned out. He'd taken his motorcycle out for a test run and left Jaye alone on the porch. Pete had insisted he'd only been gone for a few minutes. But it was long enough for Jaye to crawl out of his playpen and wander off. And Ash couldn't forgive him for not protecting their son. For months afterward, she was consumed with sleepless nights, hospital visits and endless doctor and physical-therapy appointments.

Four months after the accident, Pete left town on his motorcycle and never came back, leaving a note saying he wasn't cut out to be a father and wanted to see the world. Ash hadn't heard from him since. His mother followed a few months after he did, clearly unable to deal with the shame that her son's departure had left in his wake.

After that, Ash focused all her energy on her son, the ranch and her career. She graduated from the police academy in Rapid City and then joined the department in Cedar River. She had all the support she needed from her mother and Uncle Ted and carved out a valuable life for herself and her child. She rarely dated and didn't want to think how long it had been since she'd shared any kind of intimacy with a man.

Sheesh...too long.

Because with dating came sex, and with sex came responsibility and the potential for a relationship. And she didn't have time for that. She had too much going on. With the ranch and her job and Jaye and the kids she took in, sharing her life with someone seemed...impossible. At the very least, difficult. So, love and sex took a back seat. Or so she believed.

Since yesterday she *had* been thinking about sex. Sex that was hot and heady and scorchingly erotic. Sex that could made her senses sing and leave her breathless and wanting more.

Sex with Cole Quartermaine.

All night long.

At least, that's what she'd imagined in her dreams. She'd had a restless night and now, at nine o'clock on Sunday morning, Ash wished she could hole up in her bedroom for a few more hours and not allow reality to intrude. But it would.

I'm really attracted to you.

Cole's words echoed in her head.

She couldn't remember a man ever saying that to her before. She had gone out with a few guys over the years and even had a couple of lovers, but there had been very little heat and even less real attraction. But this—this was different. This was heat and awareness on a whole different level.

Of course, nothing would come of it. Firstly, he was at the ranch for her help with his daughter. An affair would be a distraction from that. Secondly, she wasn't about to start anything that had no future since he lived in a different state. And thirdly, it was too ridiculous to contemplate!

By the time she headed downstairs Jaye's room was empty and Ash knew he would've already had his breakfast with Tahlia and Micah and was probably outside with his great-uncle. Ricky resided in one of the smaller cabins just a stone's throw from the house, but the younger kids lived in the main house in the room next to her mother's. Uncle Ted had moved into one of the larger cabins years ago, which made him a good chaperone for anyone staying in the cabins.

Ash poured herself a coffee and buttered a piece of toast and was just about to sit down at the table when her mother entered the room. She looked up and smiled.

"Everything all right?" her mother asked.

She nodded. "Sure. I overslept. My busy week catching up with me."

"Well, you have a few days before you go back to work on Wednesday, so you have time to relax and unwind."

"I know," she said and drank some coffee. She'd planned a few days' leave to get acquainted with her new guests, but now she wasn't so sure that was a good idea. "Is Jaye with Uncle Ted?"

"No," her mother answered. "With Cole."

Her back straightened. "Why is he—"

"They're in the barn," her mother interrupted. "Tinkering with that old truck of yours, and there's a good dose of hero worship going on. The kid is certainly smitten."

He's not the only one.

Ash put on a serious face. "Cole's here to try and connect with his daughter, not to answer Jaye's million and one questions. I should probably—"

"It's good for Jaye," her mother said, cutting her off again. "And probably good for Cole, too. I think he had a rough night with Maisy. When I went to check on Ricky last night after dinner and give him his lesson plan for this week, I heard them arguing. There's a whole lot of hurt and anger in that young girl's heart, most of it directed at her father."

Ash understood the feeling. Her own father had left when she was ten years old. Her stepfather left when she was fifteen. And then Pete when she was twenty-one.

Men always leave.

She shrugged off the notion and ate her breakfast, conscious of her mother's scrutiny.

"What?" she asked.

"Exactly," Nancy said and came around the table. "What's going on with you?"

"Nothing," she said and got up. "I'm going to check on Jaye."

"He's nice," her mother said and smiled, seeming as though she knew exactly what was going on in Ash's churning thoughts. "Really nice. Don't you think?"

Ash shrugged. "What I think isn't important."

Nancy chuckled. "Oh, stop being so sensible. There's nothing wrong with admitting you like him. Or that you think he's...nice."

There was everything wrong with admitting that.

"Have you been reading Jane Austen again?" she asked and took her dishes to the sink. "You know how that always makes you sappy and sentimental."

"And I love how you always deflect the conversation away from yourself whenever I mention the idea of you dusting off that cynical heart of yours."

Ash dismissed her mother's words with a wave of her hand. "I'm not a cynic. I'm a realist."

"You're a scaredy-cat," Nancy said, grinning. "But with two failed marriages behind me, I'm probably not in a position to give advice."

"And yet, you still do," Ash said with a smile as she moved around the counter. "Can you watch Tahlia and Micah? I'll be back soon."

Ash headed outside and made her way toward the barn.

The dogs raced around with sticks and the chickens were pecking around the yard. It was a warm morning and the ranch was buzzing with sounds and scents. The goats were bleating and walking the fence line of their pen, usual behavior when they spotted someone walking across the yard. And Rodney, the five-year-old alpaca who acted more like a dog than anything else, was following Uncle Ted around near the vegetable garden. It was a peaceful scene and Ash was consumed by a sense of how much good there was in her life.

And then she heard it.

Music. Loud and awful. Some kind of heavy, brain-draining rock that hurt her eardrums.

She followed the sound into the barn and stood by the doorway. Cole was bent over the hood of her old truck, dressed in worn jeans and a black T-shirt that molded to his shoulders and showed off way too much of his gloriously well-muscled arms. And then she spotted her son, perched on an old fruit crate, about two feet away from the truck, laughing and flapping his arms in time to the mind-numbing music and clearly having a fabulous time.

Ash stayed where she was and enjoyed the moment. She loved seeing Jaye so happy. He was mostly a cheerful child, and intelligent and compliant. He had something of a stubborn streak, too. Particularly when he wanted something—like entering the soapbox-derby race at this year's spring fair. Part of her longed to let him spread his wings and enter the race. But she was scared for him and, as always, her priority was keeping him safe. If he got injured or bullied she would never forgive herself. It was better this way. Better to wait until the following year. He'd be older and better equipped to handle the risks. Sure, he was disappointed and made his feelings abundantly clear whenever he got the opportunity, but she was prepared to shoulder his frustration if it meant he was kept out of harm's way. Overprotective…maybe. But she could live with that.

"Mom!"

Jaye's voice broke through her thoughts and she frowned when she saw Cole jerk back and bang his head on the hood. He cursed loudly and then quickly apologized as he turned toward the radio and flicked down the volume.

"Mom has a swearing jar in the kitchen," her son said matter-of-factly. "Ten cents for every bad word."

Cole rubbed the back of his head. "I better start saving my dimes."

Jaye laughed loudly. "I've got a stash in my piggy bank if you run out."

Ash smiled to herself, enjoying the exchange between man and boy. Jaye's only regular male company was Uncle Ted, and although he was kindhearted, he was also busy running the ranch and didn't have a lot of spare time to spend with her son. It was nice to see him so relaxed and carefree and clearly reveling in Cole's company.

"Is your head okay?" she asked and walked toward the truck. "Not concussed or anything?"

He gave her a wry smile and his blue eyes glittered spectacularly. "Nothing permanent. Just whacked the metal plate in my skull."

"You have a metal plate in your skull?" she asked, frowning.

He laughed and grabbed the cloth Jaye was now holding toward him. "I'm kidding. About it being in my head. I do have two attached to my spine, though," he said as he wiped his hands.

Her frown increased. "Really?"

"Really. I was in an accident around ten years ago."

"I read about that," she said and forced herself to stand

back while Jaye slowly got to his feet. Helping him came to her as naturally as breathing, but she knew she needed to give him his space and independence. "It's what ended your career as a driver?"

"It did," he replied and moved around the front of the truck. "I broke my back and a bunch of other bones and spent months in the hospital."

Ash was horrified. "You could have been killed."

He shrugged. "It's a dangerous sport. I knew the risks. I had a tire blow out and lost control. It happens. But I was stubborn and wouldn't let it beat me. Then had to learn how to walk again."

"You couldn't walk?" Jaye's incredulous voice rang out between them.

"That's right, buddy. I spent a long time in hospital and then worked with a physical therapist to get back on my feet."

"I have a physical therapist," Jaye announced, clearly proud to have some common denominator with the man in front of him. "I go and see her every two weeks, don't I, Mom?" He didn't wait for her to respond. "Her name is Becca and she's really nice. Grandma says she's a cougar, though," Jaye said and then frowned. "But I don't really know what that means."

Ash gasped slightly. "Ah, Jaye, why don't you go and see if Uncle Ted needs any help with the vegetable garden."

He groaned. "But, Mom," he complained. "I'm gonna help Cole fix the truck and that's going to take—"

"You can still help," Cole said easily. "We'll work on the truck some more tomorrow. And if it's okay with you, I'd like to talk to your mom about a few things."

"About me?"

Cole shook his head fractionally. "About Maisy. You

know how I told you she wasn't feeling so great this morning?"

Jaye nodded, absorbing Cole's words as though they were gold. "Okay, I'll see you later. See you later, too, Mom," her son said as he headed from the barn.

Cole waited until her son was out of sight before speaking again. "So, about this cougar..."

Ash met his gaze and laughed. "I really have to tell my mother to stop gossiping."

"Where's the fun in that," he teased and draped the cloth over the hood. "Your brakes are fixed and the thermostat needs replacing. I've spoken to your uncle this morning and he's given me the number of a place in town where I can get the part ordered."

Fixed. Just like that. Ash had been under the hood of the old truck countless times, trying to figure out the problem. The next stop was the auto repair shop in town owned by her friend Joss Culhane—probably where Cole intended ordering the part from. She experienced a feeling of gratitude that quickly manifested into awareness when he crossed his arms, flexing muscles that were impossible to ignore. Awareness morphed into a blisteringly hot rush of lust so intense it almost knocked the breath from her lungs.

She wanted to say something. Anything. But nothing came out. It was Cole who spoke next.

"I'm sorry about last night," he said quietly. "I shouldn't have said that to you. Sometimes I speak before I think and—"

"I didn't deny it," she said, cutting him off, suddenly hot all over. The less they said about the subject, the better. "Let's just forget about it. You said you wanted to discuss Maisy? Is she unwell?"

He shrugged lightly and looked a little uncomfortable. "Ah, girl stuff, she said. Which is obviously my cue to just nod and say nothing. But if you could look in on her this morning I would be grateful," he said and sighed. "She's not exactly talking to me at the moment. She doesn't want to be here...she made that very clear."

Ash nodded, feeling a deep surge of sympathy for his daughter. And him. "My mother heard you arguing when she went to check on Ricky."

"It wasn't a new argument. Just Maisy being...Maisy."

Ash offered a gentle and knowing smile. "I'll go and see how she's doing. And, Cole," she said quietly, "thank you for spending some time with Jaye this morning. He usually only has Uncle Ted to show him things around the place."

"He's good company," he replied and smiled. "And smart, and quite the mechanical engineer. He showed me his sketches for his soapbox cart—you know, for when he gets to race."

Ash moaned a little. "He's been trying to get my agreement for the past six months."

"Last night you said you were reluctant to let him enter this year?"

"Absolutely," she replied. "He could get injured."

"Or not," Cole said as he moved around the truck and closed the hood. "I imagine it will be well supervised."

Ash knew it was. The spring fair was a popular annual celebration in Cedar River and all the competitive events were run smoothly and safely, from the rodeo to the three-legged races. But it wasn't only Jaye's physical safety she worried about, but also his emotional well-being.

"He could get...teased."

Cole wiped his hands on a rag. "He seems like a pretty resilient kid to me."

Ash straightened her spine. "Are you saying you think I should let him do it?"

Cole moved back around the truck and faced her. "I'm

saying that he's a smart kid who's sketched an impressive set of plans for a soapbox-derby cart. That's all."

Resentment licked across her skin. He didn't have any right to an opinion. And just as she was about to say as much, her irritation suddenly wavered. Because he was right. Jaye *was* resilient. And strong. And smart.

"I think I'll go and check on Maisy," she said, confused by the unexpected lack of clarity in her thinking. When it came to her son, Ash *always* knew the right road. But somehow, this man she'd known for less than twenty-four hours made her question her usual rock-solid resolve. "I'm taking the kids for a picnic down at the creek this afternoon. You and Maisy are welcome to come along."

She turned and walked away before he could respond, grateful that she didn't have to look into his eyes any longer and determined to get all thoughts of him out of her head. When she reached the cabin, she tapped on the door and, when no response came, opened it and headed inside. Maisy sat on the sofa, earbuds in, her expression like thunder.

"I knocked," Ash said when the teen scowled in her direction. She walked toward the sofa and smiled. "Your dad said you weren't feeling well. Is there anything I can get for you? Hot water bottle? Ibuprofen?"

Maisy immediately looked defensive and then shrugged. "Sure. Whatever."

Ash left the cabin and returned about five minutes later. Maisy was in the same spot, still scowling, still looking as though she had the world on her shoulders. After a few more minutes Ash had the water bottle filled, the painkillers and a glass of water on the coffee table and she held out a can of soda.

"Ginger ale," she explained. "I find it helps with an upset tummy."

Maisy took the can. "Thanks."

Ash smiled. "We're all heading down to the creek later for a picnic. I know Ricky would like the company if you're up for helping me chaperone the younger kids."

Maisy met her gaze for a moment. "Is *he* coming, too?"

"Your dad?" Ash asked. "I invited him. I guess that's up to him."

The teenager shrugged disinterestedly. "If I go, he'll go—so we can *bond*, or whatever. The counselor at school said it takes time to bond."

"The counselor is right. It takes time *and* effort."

Maisy shrugged again. "He tries too hard."

"He's your father," Ash said gently. "That's his job."

Maisy's gaze jerked upward and her expression softened for a nanosecond. "Maybe I *will* come."

"Great. I'll see you later."

Ash left the cabin and lingered on the small porch for a second, looking out across the yard. Cole was near the entrance to the barn, and then he began walking across the yard toward Uncle Ted and Jaye. He had an easy kind of swagger to his movements, and she remembered how he'd talked about the accident that had almost killed him and how he'd had to learn to walk again. It spoke volumes about his dedication and commitment. There was something almost magnetic about him…and it wasn't simply her reaction to his obvious good looks. Sure, he was handsome and had a stellar physique. But this was something else. Something more. And she was still thinking it as she walked back toward the house.

Get all thoughts of him out of her head?

Epic fail.

The creek, Cole discovered that afternoon, was actually a riverbed that Uncle Ted assured him was a premium fish-

ing spot. Not that he'd ever been much of a fisherman—
his shellfish allergy made the whole idea challenging—but
he was happy to hang out by the river's edge with Jaye
and Micah and skim stones across the water as the kids
laughed and chatted. Ricky and Ted were fishing, Nancy
had somehow managed to convince Maisy to help empty
the picnic baskets with Tahlia, and Ash was walking along
the riverbank, her dogs close by. It was an amazing spot,
sheltered by trees, and it had a wide, rocky edge. It was
the kind of place that seemed made for self-reflection. Not
that he was generally that kind of man. After the accident
and his disastrous marriage, Cole tended to live his life
in the moment, not thinking too much about the future.
Having Maisy in his life changed that, of course. He had
a child and with that came responsibility. And he wanted
it. He longed to have a good relationship with his daughter. She'd always made her feelings for him and their current situation abundantly clear. But today, things seemed
a little brighter.

Because of Ash.

He knew she'd somehow worked a little magic and put
his daughter in a better mood. It wasn't much, just a few
more words than usual from her, and a little less obvious
resentment. But it was enough to give him hope and make
him believe that perhaps things might work out and they
could make some kind of family together out of the mish-
mash they'd begun with.

He left the kids under Nancy's watchful eye and headed
along the edge, covering Ash's footprints. He was about a
hundred yards away from the rest of the troupe and about
ten paces behind her when she turned, hands on her hips.
The dogs rushed toward him and they began jumping
around his legs. She was smiling at their antics and her
hair flipped around her shoulders from the slight breeze. It

was warm out and she wore jeans, boots and a red T-shirt that managed to highlight her pale, flawless skin, bright copper hair, lush pink lips and emerald green eyes.

"So, you *are* a dog person?"

He grinned. "I think they will become a valuable lesson in tolerance."

She laughed and the sound drifted across the breeze. "Animals and children," she said and whistled the dogs to heel. "I've learned *most* of my life lessons from them."

Cole took a few strides toward her and then she swiveled and began walking again. "Do you like being a police officer?" he asked, suddenly eager to know more about her.

"Very much. It's really rewarding."

He strode out beside her. "And dangerous?"

She looked sideways for a moment and then shrugged. "I suppose it has the potential to be dangerous. I've had to use my weapon a couple of times in the last ten years— thankfully not fatally. But it's part of the job. I like that I get to help people. And, of course, having handcuffs at my disposal day and night," she said and grinned.

Warmth spread through his limbs. She was flirting. *Damn.* "Yeah, I can see how that would be advantageous."

He liked that she had a sense of humor. He liked that he could pick up the scent of her shampoo. He liked that she had continued with her walk even though he'd invaded her space without an invitation.

They walked some more and then she pointed to a small area surrounded by ponderosa pines. "There's a swimming hole through there. This time of year the water is almost warm enough for a dip. Jaye loves it in the summertime."

"He was telling me how much he enjoys coming down here."

She smiled. "We're lucky since this part of the river runs through our land. The perimeter runs along the bottom edge of the big Culhane spread—they're horse and cattle ranchers. This place is smaller, but we have water and good grazing on the other side of the river, so there's opportunity to lease some off to the neighboring ranches. But I leave that side of things to Uncle Ted." She kept walking and then spoke again. "Can I ask you something?"

"Sure," he said and kept in step.

"Why did you get divorced?"

He shrugged. "Irreparable incompatibility."

Her pace slowed fractionally. "Is that code for you'd rather not discuss it?"

"Not at all," he replied. "We *were* incompatible. Once the glow of dating and weddings and happily-ever-afters wore off, it was obvious we'd made a huge mistake. Valerie is what you might call…highly strung. We lasted two years and most of that time was a disaster."

"And now?" she asked as they continued to walk and made their way around an outcrop of rocks.

"Now?"

Her pace suddenly slowed. "I'm asking if you have a girlfriend…or significant other. Or lover?"

Cole came to a standstill. "No. No," he said and waited until she stopped moving before he continued. "And no."

Her cheeks were flushed. "I'm asking because I wanted to be prepared in case Maisy says anything about you being involved with someone."

Cole met her gaze. "Is that really why you're asking?"

She sucked in a sharp breath and the sound reached him way down low. "Of course."

He wanted to kiss her so much in the moment that his lips actually tingled. He wanted to tangle his hands into her hair, draw her mouth to his and plunge his tongue between her teeth. Heat exploded in the space between them and for one crazy second he wondered if she'd almost swayed toward him. He couldn't believe the mesmerizing effect she had on his libido. It had been a long time since he'd experienced such a strong attraction to someone.

Maybe never.

The notion rocked Cole to his core. He'd dated and slept with countless women in the past. Too many to count. Some sophisticated. Some movie-star beautiful. Some a heady mix of both. But none had possessed the hometown, down-to-earth loveliness of the woman standing in front of him. And suddenly, he was all out of resistance.

"I really want to kiss you," he said baldly.

She didn't flinch. "That would be crazy."

"I know," he said, forcing his hands to stay at his sides. "But I still really want to. I guess that's the damnable thing about being attracted to someone," he said and shrugged a little. "It can be as inconvenient as hell."

She didn't deny it, but did take a slight step backward. "We agreed to—"

"I'm *not* going to kiss you, Ash," he said quietly. "Or anything else. I just want to be straight up about this. That's who I am. I don't believe in pretense. And I think you're the same, right?"

"Right."

He nodded and then spoke soberly. "We've been here twenty-four hours and I can already see a small shift in my daughter's behavior. So…thank you. I'll take your lead and do whatever I have to do to make Maisy see that I'm not her enemy. And if that means keeping my hands to myself and taking a whole lot of cold showers, that's exactly what I'll do," he said with emphasis.

Her gaze didn't waver. She stared at him. Into him. Through him. And he allowed it. Because…he trusted her. There was something elementally honest and authentic about Ash McCune that reached him on a kind of cellular level. The fact he'd had that revelation after a mere twenty-four hours should have waved in front of him like a great red flag, but instead, he experienced a strange, almost unbelievable sense of relief and gratitude. Because it meant Maisy was in good hands. Caring hands. Healing hands.

Cole waited for his cynicism to take hold. He waited for his guard to go up. But it didn't.

Because his daughter *was* in good hands.

And so, he realized, was he.

Chapter Four

By the time they returned to the rest of the group, Ash's nerves were a quivering mess. She'd never experienced the kind of frank, unabashed honesty that she got from Cole. He didn't whitewash anything. Not the simmering attraction between them. Not the reason why it was unthinkable. It was simply put out there as though it was an undeniable fact.

"Where have you two been hiding?" her mother said and grinned as they moved around different sides of the picnic blanket.

Ash covered her embarrassment with a tight smile. "I was showing Cole where the swimming hole is," she said and looked toward a scowling Maisy. "In case you or your dad wanted to go for a dip while you're here."

"I don't swim," Maisy said, looking suspicious and unhappy.

It didn't help that Nancy was smiling and making their

absence into something conspicuous. "Well, if you change your mind, you'll know where it is. So, let's get this feast started."

The kids and Uncle Ted chatted relentlessly for the next hour, much to Ash's relief. It hid the tension that was simmering on the surface. Between herself and Cole. Between Cole and his daughter. While Nancy was smiling one of her willful little smiles that spoke volumes. Ash loved her mother dearly, but Nancy was a romantic—often a foolish romantic—falling in love too easily and too quickly. Besides her two failed marriages, there were several other relationships that hadn't worked out for one reason or another, and once the rush of romance wore off, Nancy was inevitably left with a broken heart. Ash had seen it all too often. When it came to her mother, love was always followed by disappointment.

So, her mother's penchant for falling for the wrong man over and over had made Ash wary of involvement with anyone—particularly after the disastrous way her relationship to Pete had ended. Which should have stopped her from having any kind of silly daydream about the man stretched out barely a few feet from her. Cole lay on his side on the large blanket, rested on one elbow, biceps flexed in a way that was impossible to ignore. It didn't matter that he was chatting to her son and not looking in her direction—she *felt* the awareness between them as though it were a living, breathing entity. He'd admitted his attraction to her and she hadn't denied it.

But...

There were a mountain of *buts* between them.

She wasn't the kind of woman who would take part in anything casual. She'd never had a one-night stand. Or a two-night stand. Or even a three-night stand. She didn't jump from one bed to the next. She'd had three lovers, including Pete Shapiro. She played things safe. She never lost sight of what was important—her son, the ranch, the family she'd clawed together from the rubble of Pete's departure. Thinking about Cole in that way was plain old foolish.

I know better than to be foolish.

By the time they got home it was after three o'clock. Ash helped her mother clean up the picnic things and by four she was upstairs taking a shower. It was half past the hour when she returned downstairs and found Jaye and Micah in the living room playing a video game, while her mother played cards with Tahlia. She headed to the kitchen, then pulled on her boots by the mudroom door and made her way outside. It was a warm afternoon, a typical late spring day, and it promised to be a long, hot summer. Ash loved summer. She loved the feel of the sun on her face. She loved heading down to the river for a lazy swim. She even loved cruising around in the patrol car when she was on duty and witnessing the landscape, brimming with colors of gold and green against the backdrop of perfect blue sky and in the shadow of the Black Hills. A South Dakota summer was like no other.

She looked up toward the cabins and spotted Cole sitting alone on the porch, his long jean-clad legs stretched out, his feet crossed at the ankles. Ash hesitated, but felt an almost magnetic draw toward him. In jeans and T-shirt, his belly as flat as a washboard and one hand wrapped around a soda can, he made sexy look easy.

Temptation, get thee behind me.

Still, she found herself heading toward the cabin and stalling when she reached the bottom step. "Hi."

"Hi, yourself."

"How's Maisy doing?"

He inclined his head toward the door. "Ignoring me," he replied. "So, her usual self."

"I though you both might like a tour around the ranch."

He met her gaze and slowly got to his feet. "Be back in a minute." He took two minutes and returned alone. "She's reading," he said and headed down the steps. "Looks like you're stuck with just me." He stopped a couple of feet in front of her and smiled a little. "Unless you think we need a chaperone?"

Ash raised her brows. "I don't think it's quite come to that."

Not yet, at least.

"Okay," he said easily. "Lead the way."

Ash walked across the yard, pointing to the obvious buildings—the barn, the chicken pen, the goat-and-alpaca enclosure—and then offered a brief history of the town and population.

"And you said that Cedar River used to be two towns?"

She nodded. "Yes, up until last year. But it was better for both towns to unify and pool resources—particularly things like the council offices and police department. Tourism is an important industry here, too. And O'Sullivans hotel in town is one of the best around."

"You like it here?" he asked as they walked.

"In Cedar River?" She nodded. "Yes. It's my hometown and all I know. I wouldn't want to live anywhere else. Isn't that how you feel about Phoenix?"

He shrugged. "I like the city. And my friends and family are there. So, yeah…it's my hometown," he said and smiled. "But I like other places, too."

"You've traveled a lot?"

"Some," he replied. "Europe and Asia mostly. And I spent several months in Ireland when I finished high school."

Ash considered how different her life had been compared to his. The farthest she'd ever traveled was to Denver for a friend's wedding a few years earlier. Long ago she'd had plans to travel and see the world, but her real life had intruded on those teenage dreams.

She turned and headed for the corral behind the barn, conscious that he was barely a foot away from her. Once they were around the building she whistled and then waited for the familiar clopping of hooves.

"This is Cleo," she said and pointed to the big paint mare coming toward the fence. "I've had her for a few years. She's an angel. Do you ride?"

"Nope," he replied and rested his hands on the fence. "Not exactly my kind of horsepower."

Ash laughed as Cleo swung her head over the fence. "Too bad. There are a couple of other horses we keep for the guests."

His mouth twisted. "Guests?"

"Sounds better than inmates, right?"

"I guess," he said and grinned. "So, tell me, how long have you been doing this?"

"Fostering?" She shrugged. "About eight years."

"And how did you start?"

She patted Cleo's silky muzzle. "I was on patrol and my partner and I were on what we thought was a domestic-abuse call. Turns out it was a four-year-old boy who'd been abandoned by his drug-addicted father. His mother had died a year earlier. The boy ended up in the hospital and then once he was released there was a mix-up with child services and he had nowhere to go while waiting for his grandmother to come and get him. She was coming from New Mexico and it took a few days. So, I brought him here. We had room and he needed somewhere to go. After that…" She let out a long breath. "There are so many kids who need help. Some just for a night. Some for longer, like Ricky. And then there are children like Micah and Tahlia, waiting for a permanent foster family with the hope of adoption. I guess I wanted to do something real, something that was more than lip service. Fostering felt right." She turned to face him. "But the truth is, I get a whole lot more from it than I give."

"And Maisy?"

She shrugged lightly. "That felt right, too. Joel said you needed help."

"I did," he said simply. "I do. I just—I just don't…"

"Don't know where to start?" she queried, brows raised. "You start here—today. And like I said, don't expect too much. She's a child, with all a child's insecurities and fears. And she's grieving deeply for her mother. One thing I've learned about a child dealing with such profound loss is that there is no magic cure, no words of comfort that can be offered unless they feel safe and can open their heart to trust again. But she will," Ash offered with a smile. "Once she knows you're not going anywhere and that she can rely on you, she'll open up. It just takes time and patience."

He nodded and took a long breath. "She won't talk to me about her mom. I've tried, but she closes off every time I mention her mother."

"Because she doesn't trust you with those memories," Ash said gently. "It's not so hard to understand. Don't push her. And don't be impatient."

"Patience isn't exactly my strong suit."

Ash chuckled. "I guess we're never too old to learn new things."

He rested back against the fence and crossed his arms, highlighting his biceps and wide shoulders. "So, is there anything *you* need lessons in?"

Warmth spread up her limbs. Could the man be any sexier? She tilted her head to the side a little and regarded him curiously. "Is flirting simply in your DNA?"

"That depends on how successful I am."

"Oh, I'm sure you have a good batting average."

He grinned. "Well, let's just say it's rapidly deteriorated in the last six months."

Ash didn't quite believe him, but laughed softly. "Being a single parent does tend to put the brakes on a social life. Although, I imagine you'd be considered something of a catch at the PTA meetings."

A half smile curled his lips. "Are you making fun of me now?"

She shrugged. "Maybe a little. But I think your ego can probably take it."

"What ego?" he said and looked around playfully.

Ash laughed again. It had been a long time since she'd shared any kind of flirtatious banter with a man. Years. *Forever.* She'd forgotten how it felt. And had become so wrapped up in her job and the ranch and being a mom that she'd spent a decade pretty much ignoring the fact she was a flesh-and-blood woman. But being around Cole made her remember.

And want.

"I thought I might take Maisy into town tomorrow morning," she said, flipping the subject and her thoughts to a more neutral subject. "If that's okay with you. I'd like to get to know her a little better."

"Sure," he said easily. "I promised Jaye we'd work on your old truck and then said I'd help him make a few changes to his soapbox-cart plans. I know he has his lessons in the morning with your mom, so it will be after that."

Ash bit down on her bottom lip. "Does he plan on using you as an ally in the hope of getting me to change my mind about entering this year's race?"

"Maybe," Cole said and grinned. "He's a smart kid."

"With physical limits," she reminded him.

Cole shrugged one strong shoulder. "He doesn't think so."

Ash stilled. "He's a child. And he doesn't logically understand what might happen. As his mother, it's my job to protect him from whatever I believe could put him in harm's way."

"I know."

His quiet agreement annoyed her. Because she knew it wasn't agreement. He was working her. Making her think. Making her *overthink*. Damnable irritating man.

"You think I should let him enter the race this year?" she said, eyes flashing.

He pushed himself off the fence. "He's *your* son, so it doesn't matter what I think."

Ash propped her hands on her hips. "You're right. You don't know him and you don't know what he's been through. What we've *all* been through."

"That's true," he said, so quietly Ash felt herself sway toward him a little. "But I know what it feels like to be given limits, to be told I would most likely not walk again, that a wheelchair was the best I could hope for. If I'd believed that, if I'd *let* myself believe that," he said with emphasis, "I probably wouldn't be on my feet right now. If you keep telling him that he *can't*, one day he might just believe you. Thanks for the tour," he said and walked off.

Ash stared after him, watching his sexy swagger, mouth agape. The man certainly knew how to stage an exit. She pushed down her building resentment. He didn't have a right to an opinion. He was on her ranch. Her turf. He needed her advice. Her help. Not the other way around. She wasn't about to give his words another thought.

Only...

They niggled at her. And made her think. Was she doing

the right thing by Jaye? Or was she doing what was best for her own peace of mind and not her son's happiness?

She gave Cleo another pat on the muzzle and then headed back to the house.

Cole had a restless night. The small bed was cramped and uncomfortable, and by dawn he'd had enough and planted his feet on the floor. Then he dressed and headed from the room. He made coffee, drank a cup while he stood at the kitchen sink and absently poured a second cup before he headed outside. He remained on the porch for a while, watching the sun rise, feeling the crisp morning air against his skin. Most mornings he went for a jog. He considered going back inside to drag on his sneakers, when something caught his attention from the side of the barn.

Copper hair. And a bright yellow T-shirt.

Ash...

He'd spent most of the night thinking about her. Then dreaming about her.

She was feeding the chickens and laughing at their antics and the sound of her laughter echoing across the yard had Cole instantly mesmerized. He stood perfectly still, enthralled by the image she evoked, her lovely hair shining in the morning sun, her laughter almost like a melody on the breeze.

He felt foolish thinking it.

But still, the notion lingered. He couldn't shift the image from his mind. So, he stayed where he was, watching her movements and thinking that they probably didn't make bigger fools than him.

"I hate this place."

Maisy's voice cut through his thoughts. He swiveled around to face his scowling daughter, who was standing in the doorway, arms crossed, expression as dark as thunder. "You're up early."

"Too many birds chirping around here to get any sleep. And dogs barking. And goats making weird noises."

He bit back a grin. She was right. Ranching life was very different from their day-to-day existence and luxury condo in Phoenix. But he wasn't about to make light of her complaints. He was grateful for any conversation with his daughter at this point. "I'm sure it will take a few days to adjust."

"I want to go home."

Cole kept his growing impatience in check. "It's just a few weeks, Maisy. Can you please try to—"

"Mom would never have made me do this," she said accusingly. "She'd never force me to be somewhere I didn't want to be. And making me stay here isn't going to get me to like you, just so you know."

She stomped her feet, went back inside and slammed the screen door.

He sighed heavily. Every conversation was a battle. And generally ended badly. He didn't know what to do.

"Cole?"

He turned to find Ash at the bottom of the steps. "Hi."

"Good morning," she said and propped a booted foot on the bottom step. He knew she'd heard his conversation with his daughter and her next words confirmed it. "I know this might not seem like much of a consolation, but angry words are better than no words. At least she's talking."

"I know," he said wearily and rested a shoulder against a support beam. "I'm thinking positive…promise."

She smiled and the action struck him way down low. Everything she did affected him on a kind of primary, instinctive level. Her walk. Her talk. Her damned cute smile.

"You'll get the hang of this parenting thing," she said,

her hair shining like a copper penny. "I still get it wrong and I've had nearly twelve years of practice. Remember you need to be kind to yourself, too."

"Thank you," he said quietly. There was an undercurrent of tension between them and he knew why. They'd parted badly the previous afternoon and hadn't spoken since. "I want to apologize for what I said to you yesterday...you know, about Jaye and the race. I was out of line."

She shrugged. "Forget about it."

Cole nodded. "What time did you want to go into town with Maisy?"

"Around ten," she replied. "If that's okay."

He nodded again. "I'll make sure she's ready."

Cole watched as she nodded and then headed back to the house. Once she was out of sight he returned inside. Maisy was on the couch, eyes cast downward, headphones on and clearly not in the mood for any kind of conversation. He told her what Ash said about their trip and she shrugged a shoulder in response.

"You don't have to go," he said. "If you don't want to."

"Beats hanging around here," she said.

"Don't forget you have to keep up your schoolwork," he reminded her, ignoring the contempt in her voice. "A couple of hours a day should do it." He knew she had a geography assignment due in two weeks. "Nancy offered to homeschool you while we're here, so you can catch up your classes with the other kids if you prefer."

Maisy shrugged again. "I might."

Cole pushed aside his frustration and managed a smile. "Okay, how about breakfast?"

She made a sound that was almost an agreement, so he nodded again and headed for the kitchen. Once breakfast was done and the dishes cleared away, Maisy took off for her room and Cole dropped onto the sofa and called his parents. His mother answered on the third ring and they chatted for a while and when the call ended he didn't feel quite so alone. Zara Quartermaine was a calm, loving parent who adored her children and husband. Cole was incredibly grateful for his parents and hoped he'd be as good a father as his own was. If Maisy would let him. He thought about Deanna and tried not to be resentful that she'd excluded him so completely from Maisy's life. If he'd known she was pregnant, things would have been very different. Deanna obviously had her own reasons for keeping her pregnancy a secret, but he knew he would have been there for them both. Maybe he would even have married her. Not that there was much sense in trying to rewrite the past.

It was the future that mattered.

All he had to do was get through the next few weeks and do whatever he needed to do to connect with his daughter. And to stop giving Ash McCune parental advice. So, maybe she was overprotective, but she had her son's best interests at heart. And it was none of his business.

Nothing about Ash was his business. Not her green eyes or bright copper hair, or the way she swayed when she walked or the husky sound of her voice.

He just had to remind himself of the fact every time she was in a two-foot radius.

Easy.

Maisy was surprisingly talkative on the way into town and Ash was happy to keep the conversation flowing. There was one subject that appeared off-limits though— her father—and Ash was relieved that she didn't have to talk about the man. Or think about him. He'd taken up way too much of her thinking time over the past forty-eight hours.

"We could have taken the rental car," Maisy said and scowled. "It has air-conditioning. And comfortable seats."

Ash tapped the steering wheel. Uncle Ted's battered green pickup was in worse condition than her old truck, but while hers was being repaired, it would have to do.

"A second-class drive is better than a first-class walk."

Maisy rolled her blue eyes. "I can't drive, so I wouldn't know."

"I drove my first truck when I was twelve," Ash said, eager to keep the conversation going. "My stepdad taught me how to drive."

Maisy stared directly ahead. "My mom was going to teach me," she said, her voice suddenly quieter. "You know, before she…got sick."

Ash ignored the obvious opportunity to discuss Deanna and went with her intuition. "Uncle Ted wouldn't mind if you practiced on this old girl while you're staying at the ranch. You could go down to the back pasture behind the cottages. It's a flat paddock without too many rocks. I'll mention it to your dad. I'm sure he'd be okay with teaching you."

"Couldn't you teach me?"

Ash crunched the gears deliberately. "I'm a lousy driver. Your dad, on the other hand, is a former NASCAR champion, so much better qualified for the job than me."

Maisy shrugged and then twisted the handle on the tote in her lap. After a moment, she spoke. "My mom hated him."

Ash suppressed the shallow gasp and swallowed hard, keeping her hands rigid on the steering wheel. "Did she?"

"She must have," Maisy replied. "Otherwise she would have told him about me."

"I'm sure she had her reasons," Ash said quietly, defending Deanna because she knew Maisy needed her to.

"Sometimes, when you're a mom, you have to make decisions about things. Sometimes those decisions are hard."

The teenager turned her head for a moment. "Whenever I asked her about him she said he was some rich and famous guy who wouldn't have been interested."

"But he was," she said gently. "He is. Don't you think?"

Maisy shrugged again and promptly faced the windshield. "My mom died. I had nowhere else to go. He *had* to take me. He didn't have a choice."

The pain in the young girl's voice was unmistakable and Ash yearned to stop the truck and hug Maisy close. But it was too soon. Small steps. She'd told Cole to have patience and she needed to take her own advice, no matter how hard it was to ignore the way Maisy's voice quavered when she spoke, or that her young heart was clearly broken and she felt lost and alone. Ash knew how it was to feel that ache inside—she'd felt alone when her father left, and then a few years later when her stepdad bailed. And then Pete. Thank goodness she'd had her mother and Uncle Ted. But Maisy clearly believed she had no one and that Cole had somehow been forced into taking responsibility for her.

"Sometimes, feeling like you don't have a choice can make a person resentful," Ash said quietly. "Other times, simply grateful."

"That doesn't make sense."

"Sure it does," Ash replied and decided to go a little deeper. "I was resentful when Jaye's dad left me. But really grateful that being with him meant I had a son."

Maisy clammed up for the rest of the trip, but Ash was encouraged by their conversation. Within minutes Cedar River greeted her with a familiarity that warmed her through to her bones. With a population of a few thousand, the small town sat in the shadow of the Black Hills.

Once known for its copper and silver mining, and being so close to Mount Rushmore, it was a popular tourist destination and a convenient place for commuters heading west across the border into Wyoming, or south toward Nebraska. O'Sullivans Hotel, upscale and the focal point of Main Street, was a destination that brought tourist dollars into the town. Three stories of sandstone and polished timber, with colored glass windows, it was flanked by smaller shops and retailers and had a large parking area out front. A few doors farther down they passed the museum and then the police station. Ash drove past and veered left, pulling into an empty parking space outside the Muffin Box café.

They got out of the car and spent the next twenty minutes drinking chocolate-spearmint frappés, eating pecan and maple muffins and saying very little. Then she dragged Maisy along to the hardware store to pick up a few supplies, to the library to return a couple of books and the drugstore to fill a prescription for Uncle Ted.

"Everyone knows you," Maisy said, panting a little to keep up as they were greeted by a couple of elderly women outside the pharmacy.

"I've lived here all my life," she said and ushered the teen along the sidewalk. "So have my mother and my grandparents. And I give out a lot of parking tickets," she said and grinned. "Come on, now let's do something fun."

They headed to the beauty salon and got minipedicures, including glitter nail polish that was ridiculously purple, and was also one of the few *girlie* things Ash regularly indulged in. Maisy was wiggling her toes when they climbed back into the truck around one o'clock.

"My toes look so cool. Thanks for taking me."

"I have a rule that I do one really fun thing every month," she explained.

Maisy's mouth twisted in a wary half smile. "I like that idea. But it's kinda hard to have fun with *him* watching my every move."

"Your dad?"

"Cole," she said, almost as though it was an automatic correction. "He's not my... I mean, yeah, he is my *father*. But that's not like being a *dad*."

"It's not?"

Maisy's scowl was back. But she spoke again. "I mean, a *dad* is someone who's there from the beginning. Who gets to see you being born and then grow up and then teaches you how to ride a bike and throw a baseball and—"

"Drive a car?" Ash suggested, eyes directly ahead.

She heard Maisy's reluctant shrug. "It's different, that's all."

"I only had my dad for the first ten years of my life," Ash said quietly, almost to herself. "And I'd trade those years to have him walk back into my life now, and for him to get to really know me now, and for me to know him."

"Not if he was forced, you wouldn't," Maisy said and let out a shuddering breath. "Not if he could walk back out at any moment."

Heat burned behind Ash's eyes and she blinked. Maisy's fears seemed raw and uncomplicated, and Ash experienced a deep ache inside her chest. As a foster parent, she had heard pain and sorrow countless times. She'd soothed crying children, she'd listened to stories of neglect and abuse, she'd hurt all over for each and every one. And yet, Maisy Quartermaine, with her defiant scowl and bad manners, made her ache deep down in a place Ash believed she kept hidden from the world. It was bone-deep. Soul-deep. Deeper than any child had ever delved, other than her son.

"I don't think he'll do that."

"You don't know him. Neither do I," she added, her

voice so soft it was almost a whisper. "I already lost my mom."

Her next words were unsaid, but Ash could feel them vibrating in the space between them. She stayed silent for the remainder of the trip home, sensing it was what the young girl needed. When she pulled up outside the barn, Maisy was quick to get out of the truck and sprinted toward the cabin. Ash stayed in the truck for a moment, tapping her fingers on the steering wheel, drawing in long breaths. Finally, she got out of the truck and walked into the barn. Cole was there, as she knew he would be, bent under the hood of her old pickup. She looked around for Jaye, spotted the upturned milk crate and figured he was up at the house.

Cole pulled out from under the hood and looked at her, wiping his hands on a cloth. He looked her over. Up and down. Without pretense. Without camouflage. Just one smooth, burning look, which spoke volumes. The intense awareness between them had nowhere to run. Nowhere to hide.

"You're back?"

Ash stared at him, long and hard. Everything about him was acutely masculine. Riveting. Compelling. Mind-blowing. He was a wrecking ball. And she felt as though she was standing directly in his line of fire. Without any ability to get out of the way.

"She doesn't hate you."

He frowned and his head tilted sideways a little. "What?"

"Your daughter doesn't hate you," she said again and took a deep breath.

"She said that?"

"Not in so many words. She's just terrified that she's going to lose you."

And I'm terrified, too.

Of wanting him. Of letting herself want him. Because she knew where that would lead.

To heartbreak.

Chapter Five

Cole stared at Ash and absorbed her words. Obviously, she'd had a breakthrough with Maisy. He wanted to be pleased. He wanted to be grateful. But strangely, he felt a little numb. Being around Ash was messing with his usual good sense. He didn't do messed-up. He pushed back the burst of resentment that kernelled in his chest.

"Lose me?"

She nodded and stepped closer. "Like you'll change your mind about having her in your life…or realize you don't really want to be her father."

"That's crazy," he said quickly. "I would never—"

"Fear isn't rational. Particularly in a teenager."

Cole dropped the cloth in his hands. "So, what do I say to her?"

"Nothing."

"Nothing?" he repeated. "But isn't that—"

"She needs to come to you with this."

"What if she doesn't?"

"She will," Ash assured him.

Considering his strained relationship with his daughter, Cole wasn't convinced. "How do you know that?"

"Instinct," she replied. "Intuition. A gut feeling. Experience. I just know that she will. She wants to love you, Cole. She wants to trust you. But she's scared."

He took a step closer. "Of what?"

"Of letting someone in," she replied. "Of letting *you* in. Because loving someone is scary. It makes us vulnerable. It makes us susceptible to loss and grief and no one wants to feel those things, particularly a child who is hurting as much as Maisy is. She lost her mom and, frankly, neither of us knows what that feels like."

His insides ached at the thought that Maisy was in so much pain. "Did she talk about Deanna?"

"A little. She misses her mother. But it's more than that—it's a fear of being left again. A fear of *you* leaving *her.*"

He'd never considered that to be a possibility. Maisy had made known her reluctance at being a part of his life since the first time they'd met. He'd believed her behavior was triggered by anger and resentment. But fear? The very notion his child was afraid twisted him up inside.

"I'll never leave her," he said quietly. "No matter how difficult things get."

"Exactly," Ash said and nodded. "It's a test, you see. She's pushing you away expecting you to bail. Every time she scowls, every time she calls you *Cole*, every time she disagrees with what you say—it's all a test. A test to see how far she can go, to find her limits. To see if you'll set boundaries."

"She has boundaries," he remarked. "She has curfew.

She has homework. She isn't allowed to date yet or use her phone after nine o'clock at night."

"And are there consequences if she does?"

It was a valid point. One he was forced to consider. "Well…no."

"So, no suspended allowance? No TV ban? No requirement that she comes straight home from school every afternoon?"

He shook his head, cluelessly wondering where she was going with the conversation.

"Don't you see," she said. "She needs reassurance… not with words, with actions. The only way to do that is to make sure there are consequences. If she gets home late, then she's grounded for a week. If she uses her phone when she's not supposed to, take the phone away. If you do that, she'll—"

"Hate me even more," he said, cutting her off.

"No," Ash responded. "She won't. Because she doesn't hate you. But she needs to know that you're serious about being her father. If you set boundaries, if she knows there are consequences when she misbehaves or breaks a rule, then she'll know that you're in this for the long haul. Then she'll trust you."

Cole stared at her. She was breathing hard and her cheeks were bright with color. There was so much passion emanating from her in that moment. And she wasn't being critical, even though he had a knee-jerk reaction to being told what to do or how to act.

"So, tough love?"

"Yes," she replied. "With consequences."

Cole couldn't resist the urge to move in closer. Her hair was pulled back in a clip and a few wayward locks had escaped. His hand tingled with the temptation to reach out and tuck the strands behind her ear. He could almost feel the silky tresses between his fingertips. Almost hear her sigh as his thumb slid softly across her earlobe. And then, before he could talk some sense into himself, he was doing exactly that. Touching her hair. Feeling her skin. Hearing her soft sigh as the space between them disappeared and suddenly they were so close, barely a whisper of air separated them.

"Like," he said, tracing his thumb across the skin below her ear, "if we kissed right now, there would be consequences?"

Her eyes darkened. "Sure. I'd have to hit you over the head, remember?"

Cole laughed softly. "I knew I'd regret saying that."

"That's the damnable thing about integrity," she said and smiled. "Sometimes it jumps up and bites you on the behind. That being said, you should probably stop doing that right about now."

"I should," he said, keeping his hand where it was. "I know."

But he didn't. Cole moved his hand a little lower, gently cupping her neck and drawing her closer. Heat rose and swirled between them and even though they weren't quite pressed against one another, he experienced an intense surge of desire and longing for her. Perhaps the most intense of his life. He was unused to it. And suddenly unsure of what he should do. Crazy. He *always* knew what to do when he had a beautiful woman in his arms.

But somehow, this *felt* different.

"Cole…"

She said his name almost on a sigh and his whole body responded—his skin, his blood, the very air in his chest. He felt cocooned, as though in that moment, they were the only two people on the planet. As though nothing and no one would dare intrude. There was only feeling. Only desire and awareness and a hot, burning need to take her into his arms, to kiss her beautiful mouth and feel her tongue roll against his. To have her pressed against him, breasts-to-chest, thigh-to-thigh, and then more. Much more. Everything. To touch every part of her. To feel her beneath him as they came together in the most intimate way.

"Mom?"

A child's voice cut through his thoughts and Cole dropped his hand and instantly stepped back. Jaye was approaching them, his brace making a now familiar sound as he entered the barn. Cole swallowed hard and glanced toward Ash. She was moving away from him, putting space between them as she turned to face her son.

"Hey, there," she said to Jaye, who was now at her side and waving a sketch pad in one hand. "Schoolwork all done?"

"Yep," her son replied and grinned. "I just wanted to show Cole the changes I made to my cart design. It's gonna be so cool, Mom," he said, his freckled face beaming. "I mean, when I get to *finally* make the cart and enter the race."

Cole couldn't help but smile at the boy's tactics and enthusiasm. But Ash wasn't smiling. She was frowning. And then she glared at him for a moment before she turned her attention back to her son. "We've talked about this, Jaye."

"I know," the boy said and sighed. "But I really want this, Mom. And Cole could—"

"We'll discuss this later," she said, cutting him off gently. "Don't forget you have your reading homework to do tonight. One whole chapter before bedtime." She ruffled Jaye's hair affectionately and looked toward Cole. "Maisy wants to learn to drive."

Cole's back straightened. "She's too young for a learner's permit."

"I'm not suggesting she goes driving out on the roads," she said hotly. "There's a flat bit of pasture behind the cabins. You can use Uncle Ted's truck to let her practice. That's where Ted taught me to drive when I was about her age. I thought it might be a good opportunity for you and Maisy to spend some time together."

He liked the idea. "Sure. Thanks."

She smiled but the tension between them was palpable. She was annoyed and wasn't doing a great job at disguising the fact. She obviously believed he had somehow been influencing her son to work on his soapbox-cart design. Sure, he'd talked to the boy about it, but he hadn't offered his opinion. Her attitude irritated him. Clearly Ash was adept at handing out parental advice, but wasn't keen on taking, it and Jaye's next words seemed to stick to the air between them.

"I'm not a little kid anymore, Mom. And I *can* do things."

He watched as Ash's green eyes suddenly glittered even brighter than usual and she wrapped her arms around her waist. She looked toward her son, then him, and then back to the boy, who was staring at her earnestly. She let out a long breath, turned and walked toward the door. Cole remained where he was, watching her slow amble, feeling the tension emanating from her as though it had a life force of its own, somehow connecting them in a way that startled him. She was upset. Rattled. He knew it. He felt it through to his bones. When she stopped and turned, he stilled, waiting for her to speak. Her chin was high, her eyes wide.

"All right," she said quietly and looked at her son. "You can enter the race this year."

Jaye stared at his mother in openmouthed shock. "You mean it? And I can build my very own cart?"

She nodded slightly. "Yes."

The boy pumped his fist in the air with happiness. "Yay!"

"But there are conditions," she said, sterner. "Firstly, if Cole can help you, that's great, but I don't want you monopolizing all of his time, okay?"

Jaye nodded. "Okay."

"And secondly," she said, glancing toward Cole. "You will do exactly what he says—no exceptions. Okay?"

The young boy nodded again, clearly struggling to hide his excitement. "Okay."

"And thirdly," she said, drawing in a deep breath. "I can change my mind about this at any time. Agreed?"

Jaye's head bobbed in agreement. "Yes, Mom. Can I go and tell Uncle Ted and Grandma?"

She nodded. "Sure." Once Jaye left the barn she turned her attention back to Cole. "Happy?"

Cole forced back the grin he felt. "It's not my place to—"

"Yeah, yeah," she said and waved an irritated hand. "It's not your business or your place. You didn't answer my question."

Cole shrugged lightly. "I'm happy that Jaye's happy."

"I just want him to be safe," she said quietly. "I want to make sure he's not going to be singled out because of his disability."

He nodded. "I know. The race is in two weeks. I'll still be here then. I'll make sure he's kept safe," he said, realizing the enormity of his promise, but believing it through to his bones. "Can I ask you something?"

Her expression narrowed slightly. "I guess."

"Why he doesn't go to school in town?"

She shrugged fractionally. "He did go to the elementary school in town when he was younger. But…"

"But?"

She sighed heavily. "He had a difficult time. He was…
you know, bullied…and I couldn't protect him. So for the
last few years he's been homeschooled." She swallowed
hard and then let out a shallow breath. "It's…it's simpler,
I suppose. Easier."

"Easier for who?" he asked, not quite ready to let her
off the hook. Cole watched, fascinated as her green eyes
suddenly glistened. Then she turned and walked from the
barn, her back and shoulders tight. He wondered what the
hell had made him ask such a thing, and then wondered
why she had changed her mind about Jaye entering the
race. And then, realizing he was probably never going
to understand women, he got back to work on the truck.

By dinnertime, Ash was already considering chang-
ing her decision. But the look in her son's eyes a couple of
hours earlier had broken down her defenses. Strangely, as
Jaye spoke, it was Cole's words from the day before that
had bombarded her thoughts.

*If you keep telling him that he can't, one day he might
just believe you.*

The very idea that she might be somehow hurting her
son by keeping him from entering the race had wounded
her deep down. Jaye was the most important person in her
life and she'd always believed she knew what he needed.
And the look in his eyes had told her loud and clear—he
needed this. As much as the idea terrified her.

And then Cole's question about Jaye's schooling had
rocked her foundations. The why had always seemed so
obvious. So she could keep him close. Keep him safe.

"Everything all right, Ash?"

Her mother's voice cut through her thoughts. She looked
up and saw her mother watching her from behind the

kitchen counter. Ash met Nancy's gaze and sighed. "Do you think I'm an overprotective parent?"

"Yes," Nancy replied. "But with the best intentions. You get that from your father, I'm sure. He could never bear to let you out of his sight."

Ash tossed the salad she'd made. "Until he left."

"He left *me*," Nancy said quietly. "Not you."

"He left us both," Ash said and ignored the age-old pain tightening her chest. "Can you take this into the dining room?"

"Sure. I need to get another two plates," her mother said and grabbed china from the dresser in the corner. "Cole and Maisy are joining us. I invited them for dinner."

Ash's gaze sharpened. "Oh, okay."

"Cole has asked me to help with Maisy's lessons while they're here," Nancy said and smiled. "To make sure she keeps up with the work. You know, it looks like he's getting the hang of this being-a-father thing."

"I hope so," Ash replied and flipped the lid off the potato salad she'd made earlier.

"Jaye told me about the race," her mother said. "He's very excited. It was a good call."

"One I hope I don't come to regret."

"Being a parent is never an exact science," Nancy reminded her. "Remember when you were eight and wanted that nasty little red pony that belonged to the Culhanes?"

The Culhane ranch was the biggest in the county and Ash had gone to school with several of the Culhane brothers, including Hank, who was the Cedar River police chief and his twin, Joss, the local mechanic. The eldest brother, Mitch, ran the ranch adjoining hers. Ash had always liked the Culhanes and Hank was great to work for.

"I loved that pony."

"Your father was terrified every time you went near the

thing," Nancy said, almost as though she was talking to herself. "Okay, let's get this dinner on the table."

Once her mother left the room Ash let out a long breath and continued preparing dinner. She knew Nancy didn't mean to upset her. Her mother was a kind, generous person, but sometimes she didn't have a filter for saying exactly what she was thinking. Specifically, conversations about Ash's father. Or stepfather. Both men had been important to Ash…and both had walked out. Talking about them just brought back a whole lot of painful memories she could do without.

"Need any help?"

Cole's voice. It's rich, deep timbre was becoming all too familiar to her. Ash turned and spotted him by the doorway. In worn jeans and a dark shirt, he looked effortlessly attractive and her pulse quickened instantly. She managed a smile. "Can you carve a ham?"

He nodded. "Like a pro."

Ash wasn't sure she believed him, but she handed him the carving knife and fork as he moved into the room and came behind the counter. "Thin slices. No chunks."

"Am I likely to get arrested if I mess it up?"

"Maybe," she said and raised a brow. "I may let you off with a warning, being your first offense."

He clanged the utensils. "Bring on the ham."

Ash pulled the smoked meat from the refrigerator and placed it on the counter. "Remember, slice it thinly."

"Hard taskmaster," he muttered and set to work on the leg. After a moment, he spoke again. "But, since I invited myself to dinner I won't complain about the work conditions."

"I thought my mother invited you?"

He shrugged lightly. "What were you thinking about when I came into the room just before?"

"My father."

He glanced sideways, looking surprised by her reply. Ash was surprised, too. She never spoke about her father. To anyone. Not ever. It was too hard. Too painful.

"Where is he?"

More questions. But she still answered. "He left when I was ten," she said quietly, folding table napkins to keep her hands busy.

"Why?"

She shrugged. "He was an artist. Something of a free spirit. He never really fit in here on the ranch. He wanted to paint instead of wrangling the cattle or fixing fences. There were a lot of arguments. A lot of tears. So, he and my mom got divorced and he left."

"Do you still see him?"

"No. He lives in Texas. He got married again and had another family. I talk to him on the phone about once a year."

"So, that's not him with you in the picture on the mantel in the living room? The guy in the uniform?"

She shook her head. "That's my stepdad, Alonzo. He was a police officer. Nancy married him when I was twelve. And then divorced him when I was fifteen. There were more arguments and more tears in that relationship, too." She didn't wait for him to have an opinion and spoke again. "My mother is a serial monogamist. Two broken marriages. Countless broken hearts. It was a pattern I promised myself I wouldn't follow."

"Is that why you didn't marry Jaye's father?" he asked, not looking at her as he carved the ham.

"No," she replied softly. "I didn't marry Pete because he walked out when Jaye was three years old."

He glanced sideways. "After the accident?"

She stilled. "Yes."

"Jaye talked to me about it," Cole explained. "He said he was two and a half when it happened."

"That's right," she replied. "He wandered off from the yard and got lost." She took a breath, feeling the memory through to her bones. "He fell into an old mine shaft and was stuck down there for eighteen hours. Search-and-rescue finally found him and when he was pulled out he had serious injuries. His leg was broken in three places and he had a punctured lung. Even after surgery the doctors thought he might lose his leg. But he didn't," she said and took a breath, remembering those days as though they were yesterday. "He was a fighter and pulled through. Afterward there were more surgeries and physical therapy and one specialist doctor after another. Because his injured leg is held together with metal plates and screws he needs the brace to balance out the fact that it's shorter than the other."

"And Pete?" he inquired, not looking at her.

"He left. He couldn't handle it." She took a long, unsteady breath. "He was meant to be looking after Jaye that morning…but instead he'd been tinkering with his motorcycle and then took it for a ride and forgot about his son. He left because he couldn't bear the shame of what he'd done."

"You couldn't forgive him?"

She shook her head. "I think I was so angry at first, and then so focused on Jaye getting well, I didn't have any energy left for forgiveness. By then, it was too late. Our wedding was postponed and then one day he packed his bag, got on his motorcycle and drove off. And I haven't seen him since."

"So basically, he was irresponsible and weak?"

"Yes," she agreed.

Cole placed the carving knife on the bench and turned

toward her, his hip rested against the counter. "You know, not all men are tarred the same way."

"I know that."

"Are you sure?"

She shrugged lightly, feeling awareness build between them. "My father, stepfather and fiancé all bailed—maybe that has left me a little...cynical."

He chuckled softly. "Perhaps cynicism is a rite of passage for those of us with a history of failed relationships."

Ash's brows rose sharply. "You've had more than one?"

"One divorce," he replied. "More meaningless encounters than I care to remember."

His words jarred her and Ash didn't want to wonder why. Who Cole slept with was none of her business. Still, the discomfort lingered and she asked the question teetering on the edge of her tongue. "Like Deanna?"

He nodded. "The truth is, I can barely recall what she looked like. Pretty, blond, blue eyes. That's all I remember about the woman I have a child with."

"You were young," she said and lifted one shoulder. "And most people sow oats at that age."

"But not you?" he asked, his eyes darkening.

Ash's skin prickled. "I had a child, a job and a ranch to run when I was that age. Sowing oats wasn't on my radar."

He nodded a little. "You know, having a kid changes things. And priorities. It made me realize what kind of life I want to lead and the kind of example I need to be for my daughter. I don't want Maisy to think it's okay to jump from bed to bed. Which is why I haven't been on a date in over six months." He gave a rueful grin. "Or anything else."

Ash stilled and met his gaze. And then laughed softly when she remembered how long it had been since she'd shared any kind of intimacy with a man. "You make that sound like an eternity."

His blue eyes glittered brilliantly. "It sure feels like it right at this moment."

His words were inflammatory. Flirtatious. Hot. Sexy. Everything she should ignore. If she had any sense. Which she was suddenly all out of. In a few days, he'd somehow turned her world upside down. Desire, raw and untamed and wildly galloping out of control, surged through her blood. Ash couldn't believe it. Couldn't control it. Couldn't see a way to ignore it and experienced an intense tug of attraction and longing that made her move closer, forgetting every lick of good sense she possessed. Forgetting the rules she'd set out for her life. And the handbook she'd written in her head about getting involved with someone like Cole—a man who lived in another state and who was the parent of a child she was supposed to be helping. She *never* did this. She never broke the rules. She was always in complete control of her life and her good sense.

Until Cole had walked into her life.

His eyes had darkened, his jaw was tight, his hand steady as he touched her skin. There was no denying it, no fighting it, even if she wanted to.

"Oh, hell," she whispered as his hand moved to her nape and edged her closer. "You're going to kiss me."

"Yeah," he said, threading fingers through her hair and gently anchoring her head back. "I am."

"This is crazy."

"Totally," he said, his voice raspy. "But I'm still going to do it. Maybe you should make a run for it?"

She should. "Okay."

"Or not," he said and groaned low in his throat.

Ash closed her eyes and took a breath. And waited. And finally, when the waiting was over and his mouth touched hers, she was lost, dragged into a vortex of feeling so intense she grabbed his arms for support as her knees weakened. His muscles tensed beneath her fingers, his breath sharp as he slanted his mouth across hers and coaxed her lips apart. She opened her mouth and let him inside, felt his tongue slide along hers and drug her senses with a heady, erotic expertise that was mind-numbing.

Her hands moved up his arms and found his shoulders, holding on to him as though he was a lifeline as his tongue continued its seductive foray inside her mouth. She vaguely wondered when she'd last been kissed in such a way. *Maybe never.* She pushed closer, pressed against him, his body all hard angles and muscle against her curves. It felt so good she could barely draw breath. She wondered how she'd ever look at him again without remembering the feel of him, the taste of him, the scent of him that assailed every sense she possessed.

"Oh…sorry."

Her mother's voice was exactly what Ash needed to hear, even if was the last thing she wanted. It instantly drummed sense into her head. And Cole's, too. He dragged his mouth from hers and released her, quickly putting space between them. Ash looked around his shoulder and spotted Nancy standing in the doorway. Her mother was smiling. Ash was mortified. What if it had been Jaye or Maisy who'd caught them making out?

"Everyone is getting restless in the dining room," her mother said, still smiling. "Will you two be along anytime soon?"

"Yes," Ash said and took a few steps back. "Of course. We'll be right there."

She waited until her mother disappeared before she met Cole's gaze. He was watching her with such scorching intensity it knocked the breath from her lungs. She looked at his mouth and felt her own tingle in response.

"Are you okay?" he asked quietly.

She swallowed hard. "That can *never* happen again. What if my son or your daughter had walked in here?"

"I guess we'd have some explaining to do."

"Exactly. And I'm sure that's a conversation neither of us want to have with our children. Jaye already thinks the sun shines out of you and if he saw us doing, you know... *that*, he'd start thinking that something is going on and—"

"Something *is* going on," he said, cutting her off. "We both know that."

Heat rose in her cheeks, fast and hard. He was right. But it was also out of the question. "And Maisy doesn't need any more drama in her life," she said, ignoring his words. "Things are already tense between the two of you without her thinking that we're... That—that it's okay to be..." Her protest trailed off and she took a steadying breath. "You already said you don't want your daughter thinking that casual sex is acceptable. So, we can't—"

"But this doesn't feel casual, Ash," he said, interrupting her. "Does it?"

He was right. It didn't. Ash wasn't sure what it felt like. Madness, maybe. A kind of crazy chemical alchemy that made her want him like she'd never wanted a man before.

"No," she admitted. "Which doesn't make it right. Just...complicated. And we're both too sensible to do complicated, Cole." She took a deep breath. "We can't do this. I *won't* do this. We have to show some control."

He stared at her, his gaze riveting and confronting and almost more than she could bear. A tiny pulse beat in his cheek and she was unable to look anywhere else other than his perfectly gorgeous face. Ash felt vulnerable beneath his gaze and swallowed hard, ignoring the weakness in her knees and the pounding of her heart.

"You're right," he said quietly. "It won't happen again."

Ash nodded, feeling grateful and something else. Something she couldn't quite define. Something that felt a lot like disappointment. And she didn't want to think about why. Because that would mean digging deep into the place she kept closed off, that part of herself she'd always believed was locked up as tightly as a vault.

Her heart.

Which wasn't up for grabs.

Not now. Not ever again.

Chapter Six

By Wednesday, Ash returned to work and was pleased to be back in uniform. She was on the day shift and spent the first few hours of the morning returning telephone calls and catching up on some paperwork, then going over a larceny case with the department detective, Rand Carter. Rand was a serious, brooding man who had moved from Detroit over six months ago and had become a valued addition to the department. Aside from Rand, there was a school resources officer, two ordinance officers, six full-time police officers and the sergeant. There was also a reserve patrol, consisting of a sergeant and six reserve patrol officers. With Hank at the helm as chief and Phoebe Jamison the office manager, the department was efficient and effective.

Ash adored her job and the people she worked with. Law enforcement had been her dream since high school and she was grateful to have the opportunity for a career that enabled her to serve in the community she cared for so deeply. It gave her value and purpose.

And right now an escape clause from the ranch.

She loathed admitting it to herself. And it was only true in part. She loved the ranch and the kids and her mom and Uncle Ted. She loved her friends and held deep feelings for the people of Cedar River.

But what she didn't want to do, what she was never going to do, was think about love and feelings and Cole Quartermaine in the same sentence. The same space. Not even the same stratosphere. Because that would be plain old foolish. She'd known him only a matter of days. *Five days.* Five long days of lust and awareness. Conversation that made her feel both alive and, somehow, almost lonely. And, of course, there had been one earth-shattering kiss. It was inexplicable. Confusing. Stupid.

And I'm not a stupid woman.

"You look as though you need this."

Ash glanced up from her desk. Nicola Radici was standing a couple of feet away, two take-out cups in her hand.

She laughed, delighted to see her friend, and took the coffee. "I probably do."

She'd known Nicola since the second grade and since the other woman had resettled in Cedar River a year earlier to care for her orphaned nephews and take over her family's restaurant, they had rekindled their friendship. With her friends Lucy Monero, Brooke Laughton and Kayla Rickard all finding love in the last year, Nicola was one of Ash's few remaining single friends.

"Everything okay?" she asked, spotting Nicola's frown.

Her friend shrugged. "Just having a few problems with Johnny. He's been in trouble at school. And he's stealing. He took twenty dollars from my purse yesterday."

Johnny was Nicola's ten-year-old nephew. "Do you want me to talk to him?"

"I don't know what to do," she said and sighed. "The boys have been through so much already. I know it's been twelve months, but some days it feels like yesterday."

"You're doing a good thing," Ash assured her friend. "The right thing. Once you've all worked through your grief, things will get better."

"I hope so," she said and sighed. "So, how are things going with Mr. Tall, Dark and Handsome?"

Ash shrugged and smiled a little. "I think Cole and his daughter are working through their relationship."

It was true. Maisy had thawed significantly in the past couple of days. She'd even agreed to let her father give her driving lessons on Uncle Ted's truck. She was home-schooling with Nancy and had found a friend in Ricky.

"I meant with him and you," Nicola said and grinned. "Spill."

She shook her head, silently regretting that she'd ever mentioned Cole to her friend. "It's…nothing. It's out of the question. It's not on the table."

"So, then it's serious?"

Ash laughed loudly. "No," she said. "It's simply a silly flirtation. Not serious. And definitely not going anywhere."

Nicola sipped her coffee. "Is it a geography thing?"

"It's a heart thing," she replied. "His. Maisy's. Jaye's." She took a long breath. "And mine."

Nicola's gaze softened. "Who says it will be all risk?"

"Me," Ash replied. "He's here to work on his relationship with his daughter. And I've always had a strict code about getting involved with the people who come to the ranch needing help. Every time I foster a new child, I am always torn with wanting to give them a permanent home, to love them unconditionally and forever. But that's not my job," she said and saw Nicola's understanding in her gaze. "Early on I had to learn to let go, otherwise my heart would break every time a child I'd cared for was reunited with their parents, or found a loving home with another family member, or was adopted." She took a long breath. "I love being a foster parent. I love being a *mom*. But for now, anything else seems out of reach."

It felt right to say the words and she knew Nicola understood. Her friend had become a parent under tragic circumstances a year earlier and had no time in her life for dating or anything remotely resembling a private life. They chatted for a few more minutes and almost an hour after Nicola left, and still neck-deep in paperwork, Ash took a call from the officer on the front desk saying there was someone waiting for her in reception. She stood up, holstered the pistol that was kept locked in drawer, left the office and walked down the hall.

Cole was waiting for her, seated in one of the chairs, his long legs stretched out in front, looking relaxed and way too gorgeous for her peace of mind. She thanked the young officer manning the reception desk and headed for the waiting area.

He got to his feet the moment he saw her and looked her up and down. She'd never considered her uniform particularly sexy before—but beneath Cole's penetrating gaze, the sensible belted trousers, tucked-in shirt and shiny black shoes almost felt like a gossamer-thin peignoir.

"Hey," he said finally and half smiled.

Ash couldn't help frowning. "Something wrong?"

Cole shook his head. "No. I was in town picking up a couple of parts for your truck. I thought I'd stop by so we could talk."

She didn't want to talk. She didn't want to think. She didn't want to remember the feel of his mouth against hers. Because she needed to forget and get her real life back on track.

"About Maisy?"

"No," he said, almost gravely. "Can you take a break? It's important."

Ash saw the seriousness in his expression and checked her watch. "Sure. Just give me a minute."

She headed for reception, called Hank and said she was going off-grid for half an hour and signed out on the time sheet. When she returned to the waiting area Cole was standing by the window, his back to her, looking out through the barred window.

Once they were outside she spoke again. "Where would you like to go?"

"This is your town," he replied. "You choose. But somewhere private."

She nodded and headed down the street, toward Chandler Park. It was small park with a duck pond, lots of trees, seating and plenty of privacy. They crossed the road, walked half a block and sat at a picnic table near the pond, which was shaded by a tall ponderosa pine. A couple, walking hand in hand, passed by and said hello and Ash waited until they were out of earshot before she spoke.

"Okay," she said and linked her hands together. "Let's talk."

He looked at her, elbows on the table, his chin rested on his hands. His blue eyes were unusually dark, his jaw inflexible, his breathing sharp and his expression tenser than she'd ever seen. Ash realized that he looked as though he was stuck in the center of some kind of internal crisis. He clearly had something on his mind.

"The thing is," he said quietly, his voice capturing every ounce of her attention, "I really don't want to have sex with you."

Ash swayed back in the seat and couldn't help the brittle laugh that escaped her throat. "Gee...thanks."

His brows shot up and he shook his head. "No, I mean... of course I want to make love to you. I just...can't."

"Can't?"

"Won't," he amended, his eyes darkening ever more.

Ash had never considered herself either easy *or* a prude. But that didn't mean she wanted to have a conversation about sex with the one man who suddenly had her thinking about sex. "I didn't realize I'd made the offer."

He sighed heavily. "You know what I mean."

She did. They were attracted to one another. They'd kissed. There was obviously potential for more than that. "I think we're both sensible enough to make sure that doesn't happen."

"That's just it," he said impatiently. "Usually I am sensible. Very sensible. But around you..." His words trailed off with a kind of uneasy self-derision. "Around you I don't feel the least bit sensible. I feel as though nothing else matters except *wanting* you. I don't like what that says about myself. Every time I look at you I feel like I'm an awkward, horny teenager," he said bluntly. "I hate that I can't control it, because it's distracting and putting at risk the very reason I came here."

Ash swallowed hard. His honesty was both humiliating and arousing. "I think we're both capable of putting the brakes on whatever is going on here. We did last night."

"Last night your mother caught us making out in the kitchen," he said and unexpectedly reached across and grabbed her hand. "And if we'd been alone in the house I'm pretty sure we would have ended up between the sheets. Or on the table. Or the couch. Or wherever we managed to get before our clothes were off. And right now, good sense aside, I just want to take you to that big hotel in town, book a room and spend the afternoon making love to you."

His words were off-the-charts sexy. And true. She knew there was no controlling the attraction that burned between them. He was rubbing her hand, his thumb tracing circles that were so intimate, so erotic, that Ash could have hauled herself across the picnic table and kissed him as though there was no tomorrow. But, of course, she didn't. Instead, she pulled her hand from his and tucked it into her lap.

"Then we'll make sure we're never alone," she suggested. "The ranch is filled with people, staying away from each other shouldn't be too difficult."

He shook his head. "I'm taking Maisy home," he said quietly. "Back to Phoenix."

Ash rocked back on the seat. "Just like that?"

He shrugged. "You were right in what you said. If my daughter had walked into the kitchen and had seen us together it would have been a disaster. She's already angry and hurt and I don't want to do anything that will make things worse. I have to put her first."

"Of course," Ash said agreeably, desperate to ignore her disappointed and heavy pounding of her heart. "When will you leave?"

"Immediately."

She nodded and got to her feet. He did the same and moved around the bench. It was hard to ignore how crazy it all seemed. Five days earlier they were strangers. Now, oddly, it seemed like she was saying goodbye to a friend.

"Well, goodbye, Cole. It was nice to meet you."

She held out her hand and waited for him to take it. But he didn't. He stared at her, looking so deeply into her eyes she had to fight to maintain the connection. Because inside, she was all feeling, all unhappiness, all confusion. He was leaving. She'd never see him again. Their interlude would become a brief, baffling memory. And suddenly, her unhappiness was quickly replaced by irritation. And then anger. *Stupid, egotistical man.* Did he think he was so irresistible she wouldn't be able to control herself? Did he think she was so completely sex-starved that he only had to snap his fingers and she'd jump into bed with him?

"This is for the best," he said.

Ash shrugged and shot him a sharp, angry glance. "You're probably right. But for the record, if you wanted to get me into that hotel room, you'd have to be a hell of a lot more charming and make a whole lot more of an effort. One lousy kiss isn't temptation enough to get me into bed. Have a nice life, you narcissistic, self-centered jerk!"

She turned and walked off, too angry to pay heed to the heat behind her eyes or the pain in her heart. He was leaving. And the sooner he was out of her life, the better.

By the time Cole returned to the ranch he'd cooled off a little. *Just a little.* Ash's parting comment had struck a nerve and he spent the trip back cursing himself, his wayward libido and his foolishness in coming to Cedar River in the first place. He should have stayed in Phoenix and worked out for himself how to be a father, relying on the support of his family and friends without dragging his daughter to stay at a ranch with a woman who believed he was a...

Narcissistic, self-centered jerk.

And a lousy kisser.

Right. She'd made her thoughts abundantly clear. Not that he'd ever had any complaints in that department before. In the heat of the moment he'd been tempted to prove her wrong and kiss her again. And again. Out in the open, uncaring of prying eyes.

He got out of the rental car, grabbed the small cardboard

box that contained parts for the truck and slammed the door. He was right to leave. He didn't belong on a ranch. He wasn't a cowboy. He was pure city. Yes, leaving was the smart thing to do. And then he'd quickly forget all about Ash McCune.

Oddly, that thought didn't sit right inside him, either.

He looked toward the cabin and spotted Maisy sitting on the porch with Ricky. The teens were playing cards and she was laughing and tossed a card at the boy and then another. He laughed in return and threw the pack in her lap. There was more laughter and giggles, and when he reached the bottom step he expected Maisy to clam up and glare at him. But surprisingly, she didn't. She actually smiled and pointed to the boy opposite.

"Ricky cheats," she exclaimed, laughing.

"I do not," the boy said and guffawed. "You just play badly."

"Uncle Ted already warned me that you were a cheater," Maisy said and smiled again, her face lighting up, and it occurred to him how much she looked like his youngest sister, Scarlett. And she'd just called the older man Uncle Ted? Cole looked at his daughter and wanted to capture the moment forever. She looked…happy. Like a normal, well-adjusted teenager playing a card game with a friend. "Did you two get your schoolwork done?"

She rolled her eyes and grinned. "Yes. Nancy gave us the afternoon off while she does some craft project with Micah and Tahlia. So, that means I still get cell-phone privileges, right?"

He grinned. Maisy had taken his new rule—no homework, then no phone or internet—better than he'd anticipated. "Sure."

She frowned slightly, looking at him. "Are you okay?"

Cole almost rocked back on his heels. It was the first

time his daughter had ever asked him that. "Fine," he said, holding back on telling her they were leaving in front of Ricky. "I'll be in the barn working on the truck. We'll talk a bit later."

She nodded and then took in a sharp breath. "Um, do you think we could go into town Friday night? There's a speculative fiction reading at the library. Ricky's going," she added.

For a moment, Cole thought he'd stepped into an alternate universe. Having a civil conversation with his daughter was such a rarity he had to catch his breath. And right in that moment, he didn't want to disappoint her. "We'll see," he said and left them to return to their game.

By the time he got to the barn, Cole was so wound up he could barely stand being in his own skin. He dumped the box on the workbench and rolled his shoulders. He'd had forty-odd hours to come to terms with his decision to leave the ranch. Since that crazy, mind-blowing kiss, he'd gone through every possible option and had come up with the same answer every time. The longer he stayed at the ranch, the deeper involved with Ash he would get. Leaving was for the best, the only way to ensure he steered clear of his attraction to her. He didn't want to think about how Maisy had been slowly mellowing over the last couple of days. Part of him wanted his daughter to still hate the ranch—then taking her home wouldn't cause her any grief. But he *had* seen a tiny shift in her attitude and their conversation just now was testimony to that. Who knew how far she'd come if they stayed? And how could he risk interfering with that sort of growth?

Damn. Leaving was supposed to uncomplicate things.

Cole clanged a couple of tools on the bench and swore loudly.

"Do you need to borrow a dime?"

He turned instantly. Jaye was standing by the truck, his sketch pad in his hand, a broad smile on his freckled face. The kid was always cheerful. "A dime?"

"For the swear jar," the boy reminded him and moved toward the bench. "I finished my plans," he said excitedly. "And did what you said. Here, see," he said and opened the sketch pad, pointing to the drawing of his soapbox car and outlining several places with his index finger. "And here. So my brace won't get in the way."

Cole took the notebook and looked at the design. It was impressive stuff. "Looks great. This thing will be a rocket, for sure."

Jaye beamed at him. "Yay. When can we get started?" he asked and grinned. "I know Mom said not to bug you about it, but there's only a week and a half until the spring fair."

Guilt pressed down between Cole's shoulders and he took a long breath. "Jaye, about that—"

"I'll do my schoolwork first," Jaye said quickly, cutting him off even though Cole was certain he didn't mean to. The boy was simply exuberant and excitable. "And my chores. I promise. And maybe we could work on the cart in the afternoons, once you've spent a whole bunch of time with Maisy. My mom said it's important that you guys spend lots of time together."

Cole propped his hands on his hips and smiled. Guilt and responsibility snapped at his heels and he suddenly realized exactly what he needed to do. Ash had told him that she'd learned some of her most important life lessons from children. Cole was certain he was in for some serious learning himself. He'd made a promise and he would see it through. There was no way out of it.

"Yeah," he said, conceding defeat. "Your mom is right.

And we'll get started on the cart tomorrow afternoon, say around three o'clock."

He laughed as Jaye made a whooping sound, and waited until the kid left the barn before he turned his attention back to the pickup. He had a truck to fix. A cart to build. And a daughter whose trust he needed to earn.

As for Ash… He figured the only thing he could do was stay out of her way.

Or do exactly the opposite.

When Ash arrived home that afternoon it was after five o'clock. She knew her mother would have dinner in the oven, that Jaye and the rest of the kids would be watching television in the living room before mealtime and Uncle Ted would be sitting at the kitchen table with his paper and doing the crossword. Now that she was back at work the routine would set in. It put her at ease and stopped her thinking about other things.

A six-foot-something *other thing* that she would never see again. Cole's flashy rental car was missing from the yard and she noticed her truck parked outside the barn. Mitzy and Milo were racing around the yard, while the goats and Rodney were safely in their pens and settled for the night. She eased her uncle's pickup to a halt beside her own and got out.

So, he was gone.

Good.

She didn't want to think about how the idea made her feel. She was mad at him. And disappointed. Ash hoped it worked out for Cole and his daughter. At least he'd be back in Phoenix with his family. Because family was all that mattered. She knew Jaye would be saddened that Cole had left, but she'd do what she could to make it up to her son. She'd planned on calling her mother earlier that day to let her know that Cole was leaving, but she got side-tracked by a fender bender in the middle of town, which had resulted in a DUI arrest and the ensuing paperwork.

She noticed a light on in the cabin he'd occupied with Maisy and headed for it. Tomorrow she'd strip the bed linen and air the place out. Ash climbed the steps and opened the front door. The kitchen and living room lights were on and she spotted a coffee mug on the draining board. The curtains were drawn and for a moment she thought she heard a sound coming from down the hall. Impossible, since the place was empty. Ash shrugged off the feeling and was about to walk down the hallway to check the rooms and strip the beds, when she saw a shadow emerge from the first bedroom and a tall figure strode down the hall.

Cole. Wearing only a towel hitched around his waist.

Ash was suddenly rooted to the spot and stared at him, her gaze involuntarily moving up and down, over his broad chest and flat, washboard abs and the trail of dark hair that ran downward from his navel, disappearing beneath the towel. He'd obviously just stepped out of the shower. His hair was wet and droplets of water were sprinkled over his smooth, brown skin. He had a long scar on his rib cage and she was mesmerized by every angle, every plane, every muscled line of his body. He was perfectly proportioned, all lean muscle and sinew. He had a tattoo across his heart, something Celtic and undistinguishable. And the same linked braid around his right bicep. She'd never gone much for ink. But on him it was effortlessly masculine. Effortlessly sexy. Her mouth turned dry. Her skin heated. Her breasts felt suddenly heavy.

"You know," he said when he came to a halt about three feet from her, "my face is up here."

Ash colored hotly. She'd said the same thing to him

the first time they'd met. Only then, she'd been indignant and annoyed by his blatant appraisal. Now that the shoe was definitely on the other foot, she could only manage to gape at him.

Until she finally found her voice. "You're still here?"

"I'm still here."

"I don't understand. Your rental car isn't in the driveway and—"

"It's behind the cabin under the carport." He took another step and the towel hitched a little lower. "And…I stayed."

"Why?" she squeaked out.

He shrugged his magnificent shoulders and she couldn't drag away her gaze. "Maybe I should get dressed first. Unless you prefer I remain like this?"

She shook her head. "No. Get dressed."

"Be back in a minute."

He retreated down the hall and Ash quickly turned on her heels and headed for the living room. She stood by the fireplace, knees locked, arms crossed. When he returned a few minutes later he wore jeans and a dark navy T-shirt and loafers.

Ash stared at him, keeping her arms crossed, feeling his intense scrutiny through to her bones. "You said you were leaving."

"You said I was a lousy kisser."

She gasped, coloring hotly. "I didn't say that."

"I'm pretty sure you did."

Ash shook her head. "I said that one lousy kiss wasn't enough to get me into bed. Not that the kiss was lousy. Just that the…" Her words trailed. His mouth was pressed into a tight, almost involuntary smile and she realized he was making fun. "What are you still doing here, Cole? And where is Maisy?"

"Up at the house with Ricky and Jaye playing video games." He came closer. "And I'm here because I changed my mind about leaving."

"But today you said—"

"I know what I said. I was rash. But I made a commitment to my daughter that we would stay here for three weeks. And I also made a commitment to Jaye that I would help him build his soapbox cart."

"But we—"

"I've always considered myself to be a man of my word," he said, cutting her off. "And I made a promise, one I intend on keeping."

Ash absorbed his words. "So, you're staying because of my son?"

"I'm staying because my daughter actually had a conversation with me this afternoon. A *real* conversation. And I know that it only happened because of this place... because she's found friends in Ricky and Uncle Ted and Jaye, and a kindred spirit in your mom and I believe that because of your influence, she's starting to realize that I'm not her enemy. And I'm staying because I promised a terrific kid that I would help him with something I know is important to him. Of course, if you would prefer that I left, I will certainly respect your wishes and—"

"No," Ash said quickly. "Of course not. It's just that... I mean...what about the other thing?"

"The other thing?" His brows shot up. "You mean, the you-and-me thing?"

She nodded. "Yes. It's still a problem."

"I know," he said and shrugged. "I guess we'll simply have to deal with it."

It sounded so simple. So easy. When she knew it was nothing of the sort. "You mean stay away from one another?"

"Or not," he responded and ran a hand over his jaw. "Look, there's no point in making grand statements about steering clear of one another for the next couple of weeks. This is your home. I'm a guest here. But we're bound to spend some time together and I won't disrespect that, Ash. I'm also not going to deny that I'm attracted to you. I am. Very much so. But more importantly, I want to be a good role model for my daughter. So, I'm not going to try and get you into bed. I'm not going kiss you. Or touch you. Or do anything that isn't strictly platonic. Unless," he said softly, his voice holding her entire attention, "you want me to. It's your decision. Your call."

Her decision? She wished she had that elusive frying pan to smack him over the head. "You're saying that it's my decision if we do or don't have a fling while you're here?"

"Exactly."

"Because you want to spare your conscience?"

"Because I don't want to lie to you," he replied. "I like you. And I'm very attracted to you. And I want to make love to you. But we both know that whatever happens, it's temporary. We live in different states and have different lives and a long-distance relationship isn't viable."

"We've known one another for five days," she reminded him. "It's a little premature to be using words like *relationship*."

He hitched his hands to his hips. "I don't know... Tell me, have you ever had this kind of intense physical attraction to someone before?"

It was a ridiculously arrogant question, but she couldn't deny it. "No."

"Me, either," he admitted. "So, if something happened between us, we'd both have to agree that it would be just for now, just for this brief span of time."

"But it won't happen," she said, swallowing hard. "And

if it did, it would have to stay just between us, because it might lead to some people getting certain ideas…like my son. Or Maisy. Neither of them need any more confusion in their lives."

"You're probably right."

She took a breath, felt his burning scrutiny through to every molecule she possessed. "So, it's settled. No fling. No…anything."

"If that's what you want."

She tensed. "I love how you get to have all the scruples and integrity here."

"And cold showers," he reminded her.

She let out a brittle laugh. "So, you're handing me all this power?"

"Yep," he replied. "Around you I *feel* powerless, Ash. You're beautiful and smart and you literally take my breath away."

It was a startling admission. No man had ever said that to her before. But, then again, she'd never met a man like Cole before. He was honest and forthright. Strong and fearless. He was exactly the sort of man she'd imagined she might fall for in her secret dreams. In the very depths of her heart she'd longed for the fairy tale—for a man who had strength in his character and integrity imprinted in his DNA. Someone she could rely on. Lean on. Trust and honor for the rest of her days. Someone who would make her feel whole and take away her fears of being abandoned. It was a lot to ask. A lot to expect. And in her bitterness and cynicism, she'd never really believed a man like that existed.

Until now.

"So, it's settled—you're staying?"

He nodded. "I'm staying. It's what my daughter wants. What she needs."

Ash sucked in a long breath. "Okay. We'll keep it simple. You help Jaye with his cart, I'll help Maisy work out that you are not her enemy. And maybe we'll end up being friends when this is all over."

"Maybe," he said and smiled. "My daughter has made plans for Friday night, at the library."

"The reading," she said, remembering that Nancy had mentioned something about it. "Sure. Ricky will be there."

He nodded. "I thought we might take the rest of the kids into town for dinner."

She stilled. "That sounds like a date?"

"A purely platonic date," he replied. "Well chaperoned."

She could do that. He'd made it clear that he wanted her. He'd also made it clear he wouldn't do anything about it. And Ash had always considered herself to be a woman of great self-control and high morals, so there was no problem she could foresee. A chaperoned, platonic date wouldn't test either of them.

Would it?

Chapter Seven

By Friday afternoon, the bones of Jaye's cart were well on the way. Cole had scrounged around the ranch for materials and then bought what else he needed from the hardware store in town. Curbing the kid's enthusiasm was impossible and by the second afternoon it had become contagious. Micah and Ricky helped out once their lessons were done for the day, while Maisy and Tahlia hung around the barn, pretending to ignore the project completely, with his daughter making some eye-rolling comment about *macho conditioning*.

He liked how all the kids got along. There were a few minor squabbles, but nothing serious and Maisy was becoming more talkative and responsive with each passing day.

While Ash stayed away from the barn.

They'd hardly spoken since Wednesday and Cole couldn't ignore how much he missed talking with her.

She'd spent the previous evening with Maisy, watching a chick flick that he knew would have made his eyeballs bleed, so he'd stayed in the cabin and answered emails and spoken to his sister about some contract negotiations for a new team sponsor. He was surprised by how little he missed his job and on self-reflection realized he hadn't been truly happy with his career for a while. Since his divorce, certainly, and probably before that. Since he'd stopped driving. Managing the team had been the obvious move and one he'd planned on after he'd finished racing. But the accident and forced retirement had brought it on ten years before he was prepared for it. Still, he had a lot to be grateful for. And *unhappy* wasn't really the right way to describe how he felt. Dissatisfied, maybe?

It gave him a lot to think about. To wonder about. He'd been born into the racing scene. He'd never questioned his decision to drive and when that was taken from him, Cole literally changed gears because he had to, convinced that since racing was in his blood there was no other option.

But now, he wasn't so sure.

"You look nice, Mom. Don't you think, Cole?"

He snapped his attention back to the present. Ash had stepped out onto the porch, dressed in a short denim dress and sexy pink cowboy boots. And he was done for. For a second he forgot to breathe. Forgot his promise to *stop* thinking about her in that way. Jaye was standing beside him, leaning heavily on his brace, while Micah and Tahlia were already waiting in the car. It was nearly sundown, but there was still enough light that Cole could see how stunning she looked. It had been forty-eight hours since they'd been this close to one another and as he dragged in a breath, he realized just how much seeing her meant to him.

Too much.

"Yes," he said to Jaye. "She certainly does."

She met his gaze and smiled and his insides did a foolish loop-the-loop. He'd made the right decision in staying, but damn if it didn't feel like the most difficult thing in the world right at that moment.

"I'm ready," she said and came down the steps. "I see my mother already left with Maisy and Ricky?"

He nodded and opened the front passenger door for her while Jaye climbed into the back seat. "It was good of her to take them. I think my daughter has found kindred spirits in Nancy and Ricky, and their joint love of books."

She smiled and slipped into the seat, then clipped the seat belt as he closed the door. He thought about how much it felt like they *were* on a date, despite the three kids in the back and the fact they were going to be strictly platonic. Cole moved around the other side, started the engine and glanced at her, riveted by her beauty and the relentless effect she had on him.

"Everything all right?" she asked.

"Fine," he said and released the parking brake. "Just fine."

JoJo's Pizza Parlor was a busy place, with checked tablecloths and bunting in the color of the Italian flag pinned around the walls and empty Chianti bottles suspended from the ceiling. It was a comfortable, clean family-style restaurant with a discreet bar in one corner, a piano in the other and a small area with a few arcade games clearly designed to keep kids entertained. He'd booked a table and they were all seated at a booth in a cozy spot near the back. Ash introduced him to her friend and the owner, Nicola, a pretty young woman with a riot of brunette curls and who gave him a curious and deliberate once-over and then took their drinks order.

"She seems...nice," he said as Ash settled in the seat

opposite. When their knees touched he almost jumped out of his skin.

She met his gaze, smiling, as though she knew exactly the effect she had on him. "She is. Nicola inherited custody of her two young nephews last year when her brother and sister-in-law died. She moved back to Cedar River to take care of them and run this place."

"Another real-life angel then," he said quietly. "Like you."

"Angel?" Her brow rose. "I don't think I've ever been called that before."

Cole glanced toward Micah and Tahlia, who sat beside him on the bench, happily chatting to Jaye, who was next to his mother. "Oh, I think that's a fairly accurate depiction. I don't think you fully comprehend how much you do."

She looked a little embarrassed and smiled. "They complete my life. Kids have a way of doing that."

Cole nodded. "I'm starting to realize that's true."

She picked up the menu and looked at him over the top of it. "So, you're getting used to this parenting thing?"

"I think so. Maisy has been more talkative the last couple of days. I mean, she still hasn't opened up about her mom or talked about anything deep, but I'm hopeful she will over time. We've been watching television and I've been teaching her how to play poker."

Her brows shot up. "Poker? Really?"

He laughed. "Only so she can beat Ricky. He cheats."

She rolled her eyes comically. "I'm so pleased things are improving."

"Me, too," he admitted. "For a time there I thought it would never happen."

Their drinks arrived and once the kids had taken sips of their soda they pleaded to go to the gaming area. Ash nodded her approval and he knew she would keep a watchful eye on them from their position.

"You're a mom twenty-four seven," he said and drank some of the imported beer he'd ordered. "Right?"

"Habit," she replied and laughed a little "Which is why I've probably never had time for romance."

"Never?"

She shrugged. "Nothing serious. Not since Pete. I suppose at some point I'll have to accept the fact that I'll probably never get married."

The idea of her married jolted his insides. He didn't want to think about it. And he certainly didn't want to think about why it bothered him so much. "You're still young. You have time to meet someone and have a big fancy wedding."

"Like you did?" she asked.

Memory of his ridiculously grand, absurdly expensive wedding to Valerie flashed in front of his eyes for a brief, painful second. "And we both know how that ended."

She sipped her soda and then met his gaze. "Who left who?"

"In the end it was a mutual parting of the ways," he replied stiffly.

"Did you love her?"

"I thought so at the time," he said and sat back in the seat. She was clearly curious and since Cole found talking to her oddly relaxing, he kept going. He rarely talked about his broken marriage, but the words came out before he could stop them. "Valerie was beautiful—runway-model beautiful, if you know what I mean. Perfect in every way. Except the ways that counted most." He tapped his chest lightly. "In here. She was self-absorbed and self-destructive. She married me for my money and connections and made that very clear when I filed for divorce. She gambled," he explained, and saw the sympathy in Ash's expression—for the first time since the divorce he felt as though he was being truly heard. His friends and family always seemed to offer sage advice and counsel about his failed marriage. But Ash McCune merely listened. And that, he realized, was enough. "She drank. And I'm almost certain she was unfaithful. She was like a facsimile of beauty and perfection. Sometimes I wonder if I only saw what I wanted to see in the beginning. Because I thought it was time I settled down and got married."

"I'm sorry for your loss."

Cole looked at her. "Thank you. It's funny, but most people tell me I should be grateful we were only married for two years and didn't have children. As though that's some kind of bonus or consolation. It's not. It just makes the whole thing feel like a greater failure."

She nodded and her green eyes glittered brilliantly. "I get the same thing said to me about my relationship with Jaye's father. You know, how I had a lucky escape—that kind of thing. The thing is, I've never felt lucky, only sad. For me, for my son…and even for Pete."

"He was a fool to let you go."

"Yes, he was."

Her eyes shimmered brightly and Cole realized she was on the verge of tears. "I'm sorry, Ash. I didn't mean to upset you."

She blinked. "You didn't. I think you're probably one of the few people I've met who actually *get* me."

Ditto.

A waitress approached to take their order and once they'd made their selection the mood had shifted, becoming lighter. They talked about the upcoming spring fair and Jaye's cart and they shared stories about growing up in a city versus small town, and by the time the pizzas arrived the kids were back at the table. Cole figured they looked like an eclectic bunch—with Jaye's shock of red hair, Ash's fair complexion compared to his own brown skin and Micah and Tahlia's Native American heritage, they probably were a postcard for a blended family.

He liked the idea, though. Being around Ash made him think about family more than he usually did. And marriage. And children. And a whole lot of things he'd thought he'd become too cynical for.

Afterward, when the pizza was eaten and the kids each consumed a bowl of ice cream, Ash suggested they walk around town for a while before they headed home. Since it was still early, Cole didn't mind. Maisy wouldn't be back until after nine o'clock and he liked the idea of spending more time with Ash and her kids.

It was a warm night and there were several other families out walking. Ash appeared to know everyone who passed by. A couple around their own age approached with a baby in a stroller, and she introduced them as Tyler and Brooke Madden. They lived on a small ranch not too far from Ash's and he owned a law practice in town. They chatted for a few minutes and once the other couple left they continued their stroll up the street, while Tahlia and Micah raced on ahead, running off the sugar from their sodas and ice cream. Jaye trailed them, slower, but still laughing. Cole watched Ash follow her son's every move. There was no doubt that she cherished her child, and she looked as though she wanted to call him back. When Jaye stumbled a little her pace quickened and Cole suspected she was finding it difficult to *not* rush forward and help him. But she didn't.

"You seem to have a lot of friends in this town," he remarked as they walked side by side.

"I guess I do. Don't you know a lot of people in Phoenix?"

He shrugged. "I have a few close friends. And yes, I know a lot of people, but they're more acquaintances than friends. And I haven't met most of the people in my apartment building, let alone know them by name."

A couple of teenagers suddenly sped by on skateboards and Cole automatically called for the kids to watch out and then reached for Ash, grabbing her hand and pulling her close. The teens apologized and quickly rushed off and Ash looked up at him once she'd checked that Jaye was unharmed.

"You have quick reflexes," she said, but didn't pull her hand away.

"Quick reflexes are a must when driving around a track at two hundred miles per hour," he replied as they continued walking, hands still together. Cole linked their fingertips and had a vague thought about how long it had been since he'd held a woman's hand and simply walked down the street.

"Do you miss it?" she asked quietly.

"Yes," he said and then sighed. "You know, I don't think I've ever admitted that to anyone before."

"Because you don't want pity?" she queried way too intuitively. "Since you can't drive competitively anymore?"

He nodded. "Yes. Too many broken bones. Too many surgeries. Too much risk. I had to make a decision—drive or walk."

"It must be hard to give up something you love doing. I mean, if I was told I'd never be able to serve as a police officer again, I'd be devastated. Of course, I know I'll have to retire at some point."

"Maybe you'll get to keep the handcuffs," he teased.

She laughed. "Maybe. I'll let you know."

His cell rang, interrupting them, and he reluctantly released her hand and pulled the phone from his pocket. He recognized his mother's number instantly and took the call, speaking to her for less than a minute.

After he ended the call he looked at Ash. "That was my mom. Looks like they want to come and visit."

Her eyes widened. "Here?"

He nodded. "Yep. They'll be here next Friday. All of them. I'll book them into O'Sullivans."

"They can stay at the ranch if you prefer."

Cole shook his head and chuckled. "One thing you don't want is a house full of Quartermaines, believe me."

"Oh, I don't know," she said and laughed softly as they continued walking. "I kind of like the ones I've met so far."

"My family really is the best," he told her and grinned. "But they can be a little overwhelming all together. They can stay at the hotel, my mom can see that Maisy is just fine and then they will be on their way."

"I'm looking forward to meeting them."

Foolishly, he was looking forward to Ash meeting his family. He knew his mother would fall in love with her.

Just like I'm falling in love with her...

Cole shook off the thought and cursed himself for being so stupid.

By the time they were back at the car it was close to eight thirty. Once they were home, he waited by the bottom step until the children climbed the stairs and then said good-night to Ash.

"I had a nice time," she said, looking lovely in the moonlight. "Thank you."

"See, we can do platonic."

"Except for the hand-holding."

Heat slashed his cheeks. "It was strictly platonic handholding," he assured her. "Promise."

She laughed and the sound echoed around the yard. "You really are a lousy liar, Cole."

He raised his palms. "Bad liar. Bad kisser. So many faults."

She laughed again, so sexily he had to catch his breath as he watched her turn and head up the steps. Before she reached the top step she turned around and said his name. "You know, it's not that I have a lot of experience for comparison, but if you must know, I think you're one of those men who are good at everything."

As he watched her walk through the doorway and then disappear into the house, he was smiling. And when he turned to head back to the cabin, he was laughing. And thinking that he liked Ash McCune a whole lot. He more than liked her. And that meant he was completely and utterly screwed.

On Monday afternoon Ash got home around two o'clock to discover that Ricky was packing his bags. His older cousin from Tucson had arrived and offered to have the boy go and live with him and his wife. Ash supported his decision, knowing how important family was. But as his foster parent she still had an obligation to ensure his well-being.

"Are you sure this is what you want?" she asked.

He shrugged his lanky shoulders. "I can't stay here forever."

"You can stay here for as long as you need."

Ricky's eyes filled with tears and he swallowed hard. "I know I can...but I can't. I'm nearly eighteen and gotta make my own way. We both know my folks are never gonna accept me. But my cousin, he's cool, and I talked with his wife today and she sounds cool, too."

So, it was settled. Ash talked at length to his cousin, a well-spoken man in his late twenties who was a firefighter and quickly realized that Ricky would be well cared for. She contacted his case worker and explained the situation. Since he would legally be an adult within a few months, by late that afternoon the teenager had given her a hug and left with his cousin, waving and promising to keep in touch. She hoped he would, but also understood he needed to concentrate on his new life and not dwell on the past.

Saying goodbye was always difficult and saying it to a child she had grown to care about always took a little piece of her heart. Ricky's departure affected everyone differently. Jaye had developed a strong bond with the other boy and she knew her son would miss his friend. Micah and Tahlia stayed quiet in the living room with Uncle Ted and her mother was wiping away a few tears in the kitchen.

Figuring the best thing to do was carry on as normal, Ash headed for Cole and Maisy's cabin to invite them to the house for dinner. She tapped on the jamb and the door swung back a few moments later and Cole stood beneath the threshold. His jaw was tight, his shoulders bunched, his mouth pressed into a grim line.

"Everything okay?"

He shook his head. "Not exactly. Maisy wants to leave."

Ash frowned. "But things have been going so well."

"Until today." He opened the door wide and stepped aside to let her pass. "Maybe you can talk with her. She's in her room…packing."

Ash let out a long breath, grabbed his arm and held on for a moment. His skin was warm and the touch between them was electric. He looked so achingly unhappy and she longed to fall into his arms and offer comfort and support. Instead, she nodded, dropped her hand and then headed down the hallway. The door to Maisy's room was open and she watched for a moment as the girl refolded a shirt several times before placing it in her suitcase.

There were a couple of books on the bed—old sci-fi novels she knew had belonged to Ricky—and she quickly figured out why the teenager was so upset. Ash said her name and Maisy looked up, her blue eyes filled with a kind of inexplicable rage.

"You know, it's okay to be angry."

Maisy shrugged. "I'm not. I just want to go home. I hate it here."

Ash walked into the room and sat on the end of the bed, hands in her lap. "I understand. If I was away from my friends and family, I wouldn't want to stay away for too long."

Maisy's expression darkened. "I don't have a family."

"Sure you do," she said gently. "I mean, you have your dad, and I hear you have grandparents and two aunts back in Phoenix. In fact, I believe they are planning to come here next weekend. It's lovely they care about you so much that they'd come all this way for a visit. I think that's why Ricky decided to go and live with his cousin, because he wanted to be with his family."

She shrugged again and tossed a pair of jeans into the case. "I dunno. He can do what he likes."

Ash smiled. "People generally do. And as long as we don't hurt other people in the process, it mostly works out okay."

Maisy made a grunting sound. "Do you think so?"

Ash nodded. "I've been a foster parent for a long time and when one of the kids leave it's always difficult at first."

"Then why do you do it?" she said angrily and thrust a sweater into the case.

"Because the happy times make the hard times worth it," Ash replied. "Ricky was here for nearly eight months and I grew to care for him a great deal. We all did. But at some point, he was always going to leave."

Maisy stopped tossing clothes and looked at her. "Why?" Her bottom lip trembled. "Why do people always leave?"

Ash shimmied around the edge of the bed and moved closer to her. "People leave for lots of reasons. Sometimes it's because they can't stay." She hesitated for a moment, knowing she was treading in dangerous waters. "Sometimes it's because they die."

She watched as Maisy's expression suddenly shifted from rage to despair. Ash remained perfectly still, waiting for the young girl to speak. Tears filled Maisy's bright blue eyes and Ash swallowed the lump of emotion in her throat. And then the teenager dropped onto the bed beside her and collapsed in her arms.

"I miss my mom so much," Maisy sobbed, her despair palpable.

Ash held her tightly. "I know you do," she said soothingly. "I know."

"Why did she leave me alone?" Maisy wailed, her voice muffled against Ash's shoulder.

"Oh, honey," Ash said and stroked her hair. "You're not alone. You'll never be alone. Not ever. You've got your dad and your grandparents and—"

"He hates me," Maisy said and shuddered. "I know he hates me. I know he wishes he'd never found out about me."

"I don't think that's true, honey," Ash said as she held her tight. "But I think he thinks that you hate him."

"Sometimes I do," she admitted and cried some more. "Because being with him means that my mom is never coming back and I—I just wish she hadn't got sick. It happened so quick and there were doctors and hospitals and so much going on we didn't have time to say goodbye. Not really. And then she was gone and I was told I had to go and live with someone I didn't know. Someone who didn't even know I existed. And no one asked me what I wanted."

Ash looked up and saw Cole standing in the doorway. The pain in his expression spoke volumes and she desperately wanted to make things right for him. For them both. But in that moment Maisy needed her more. She was a child grieving for her mother and needed comfort and reassurance from another woman. Ash held up one hand, telling him without words that he should leave them alone for the moment. She felt bad for him through to her bones and managed to nod reassuringly, patting Maisy's back as the girl sobbed against her. He lingered for a microsecond, clearly torn between wanting to console his child and doing what Maisy needed the most. When he turned and left, the anguish she saw on his face nearly broke her heart in two.

She stayed with Maisy for close to an hour. Holding her. Talking to her. Reassuring her. Calming her through endless tears. Finally, after she placed the suitcase on the floor and left Maisy to rest, Ash was more emotionally drained than she could remember feeling for a long time. She closed the bedroom door softly and walked down the hallway. Cole was in the lounge room, sitting on the sofa, his face in his hands.

He looked up and met her gaze. "How is she?"

Ash nodded. "Resting. Exhausted."

"And you?"

She moved around the coffee table and sat down. "I'm okay. How are you feeling?"

He shrugged loosely. "Helpless."

"It will pass, I promise," she assured him. "This is a good thing, Cole. What happened with Maisy is exactly what needed to happen. She had to get those words out and really *feel* them."

"Without me?"

Ash perched on the edge of the seat. "Yes…this time. Because there was no risk saying them to me. She had nothing to lose. And it wasn't about excluding you or making you feel helpless, even though it probably felt that way."

"It did," he said flatly. "It does. But all I really care about is Maisy. I want her to be happy and to know she can rely on me. And to know that I truly do want her in my life."

"You will get that chance. This is a big step. But it's important to have patience and let her keep taking these steps at her pace. I think Ricky's leaving pushed a button inside her," Ash explained, her voice as quiet as she could make it. "And there will be other things, other buttons along the way, and each one will be another step toward you and to her accepting you as her father."

He sprang to his feet and paced the room, coming to a halt by the fireplace. He dropped his hands to his sides as he let out a long and weary breath. "I do love her, you know."

"I know."

"At first, I wasn't sure if I would," he admitted, and she watched him swallow hard. "I thought, how can I care about a child that I don't know—a child I never witnessed growing in her mom's belly? A child I never got to see come into the world. Whose first cry, first steps, first words, first tooth were all things I missed. A child who was grown up and had her own mind and ideals." He sighed heavily. "And then I met her. I met this angry, lost girl who had eyes just like mine and I felt an overwhelming connection that was inexplicable to me. And I realized that none of what I had missed actually mattered." He placed a hand to his chest. "Because she's a part of me. My child. I helped make her and she's incredible. And so what if I missed out on the first fourteen years? With any luck I'll get to be there for the next fifty. I'll get to see her graduate high school and college. And maybe one day I'll get to walk her down the aisle and then she'll have children of her own. All I know is, I want to be there for all those things."

Ash's chest tightened and she got to her feet, walking toward him. Once they were barely a foot apart she reached out and touched his face, cupping his strong jaw, feeling the pulse beating wildly in his cheek beneath her palm.

I could fall in love with this man.

The idea terrified her. She'd spent a decade avoiding feelings. Avoiding the kind of instinctive pull she felt toward Cole. The crazy thing was, they weren't in a relationship. They'd shared one kiss. And yet, she experienced an intimacy and connection toward him she'd never felt before. If she believed in reincarnation, Ash would have sworn they'd somehow known one another in another life. Another time. Another dimension.

I am falling in love with this man.

She moved closer and he roped an arm around her waist, pulling her against him. Ash pressed her face into his chest, felt his heart pounding beneath his rib cage, inhaled the scent of him that assailed every sense she possessed. He rested his chin on her head as his other arm came around her. They didn't move. Didn't speak. Didn't do anything for what seemed like ages, but was probably barely minutes.

She'd been strong and independent all her life. She ran her ranch, raised her son, watched over other people's children and protected her town. She'd never really longed for the safety of a man's arms, because she hadn't truly believed it existed. But standing with Cole, feeling the heat and strength of him seep deeply into her, Ash knew she was a fraud. She did want it.

She wanted *him*.

Ash pulled back a little and then pushed up on her toes and kissed his cheek. "I'll see you tomorrow," she said, forgetting her plan to invite them to dinner. Maisy needed to rest and Cole needed to stay close to his child.

He nodded. "Okay. And thank you…for caring about my daughter. It means a lot to me."

Emotion burned her throat. "Good night, Cole."

"Good night."

Then she bailed, before she did something foolish— like admit she was halfway in love with him. And on the verge of falling the rest of the way.

Chapter Eight

"I think you left the gearbox back there."

Maisy scowled and crunched the gearshift once more, then turned Ted's old truck into a sharp arc and narrowly missed the fence. On the third day of driving lessons in the pasture behind the main house, she had at least managed to drive the vehicle for a few minutes without stalling it with an uncomfortable jerking motion. Cole hung onto his patience and braced his back for the inevitable and abrupt halt that was about to happen when she pressed the gas and clutch at the same time. Still, he had to give the kid credit for perseverance and commitment...until the truck stalled again and he called it quits. They switched seats and he drove the pickup back toward the barn.

"I think I'm improving," his daughter said and planted her hands on her hips. "I only stalled five times today."

"Six," Cole said and held up one hand while he rubbed

the back of his neck with the other. "Not that I was counting."

She laughed. "I'm sure I'll get the hang of it by the time I'm old enough to get my learners permit."

Cole's brows rose. "You mean I've only got another year or so of this?"

She laughed again and he liked the sound. She'd done a lot of laughing in the past couple of days. And talking. Not so much to him, but to Ash. They had developed a bond and he didn't mind. As long as his daughter was talking to someone, he was happy.

"Can we do it again tomorrow?" she asked.

Cole grinned and rubbed his neck again. "Sure."

Maisy laughed. "I'll try and do better."

"You're doing fine," Cole assured her.

"I might be as good as you one day," she said and raised one brow questioningly.

"You just might. You've got the basics down," he said and nodded. 'The rest will come with practice."

"It's probably a DNA thing," she said and offered him a smile that seemed so sincere, Cole had to swallow the tightness in his throat. "You know, since driving is in my blood."

He stared at her and then smiled warmly. It was the first time Maisy had acknowledged that they shared anything and he was shocked and overjoyed by her admission. It was a small step…but an important one. Once she headed back to the cabin, Cole then spent the next few hours in the barn with Jaye, putting the finishing touches to the cart. The kid was beyond excited and badgered him for a trial run. With Ted's help, they found a suitable spot down by the river they could use as a practice strip. Jaye crashed the thing on the first run and Cole almost lost the contents of his stomach for a moment when he thought the boy might be injured. But Jaye was a tough little dude, and even though he had a cut lip and a grazed knee, he insisted they keep practicing. They stayed out for another hour and by the time they got back to the barn it was past four o'clock. Cole sent Jaye off to the house to get cleaned up and he was tinkering with the cart when he heard Ash's voice behind him.

"So, do you want to tell me why my child is bleeding?"

He quickly covered the cart with a tarp as he turned to face her. Jaye had made it very clear he didn't want his mother to see it before the big day. She'd agreed, albeit a little uncertainly, but with a smile.

Only she wasn't exactly smiling now.

"He crashed," Cole said and looked her up and down, thinking how sexy she looked in her uniform. "But don't worry, he's okay."

"Don't *worry*?"

He grinned. "He's a tough kid. And crashes come with the territory."

"Great," she said sarcastically. "I feel so reassured."

"You should. Jaye designed a good cart."

She stepped closer. "I think I should see it, to put my mind at rest."

"No chance," Cole said and stood in front of the tarp. "He wants it to be a surprise."

"I could insist."

"You could," he said and grabbed her hand. "But you'd have to get past me first."

She swayed toward him a little. "Since I have all the power in this relationship," she reminded him, "I'm pretty sure I could have you doing exactly what I wanted in about ten seconds flat."

Cole curled their fingers together. "No chance," he said. "Five seconds, for sure."

She laughed. "You are an outrageous flirt, you know that."

He rested his behind on the bench and pulled her closer. "You're the one coming in here dressed all hot and sexy."

She laughed and looked down. "You have a serious problem if you find this outfit sexy."

"On you, Officer McCune, I'd find a flour sack sexy," he said and did his best to ignore how all the blood in his system seemed to suddenly be rushing to one part of his anatomy. Her body curved into his and there was no denying the desire between them.

"You know, this doesn't feel particularly platonic," she said wryly.

"No," he said and grasped her hips, urging her closer. "It feels good, though."

She laughed and the sound struck him down deep. Her laugh was like a tonic. Since Ricky's departure and Maisy's opening up to Ash, things had shifted between them. Subtly at first. For days, they'd been skirting one another. A look. A touch. It was all they needed to do to heat his blood and make him want her like he'd never wanted a woman before. And there had been flirting...lots of flirting. Maybe because they both knew it couldn't go anywhere, but they were both powerless against the attraction they felt. And in his arms she was a perfect fit against him, all soft curves and loveliness to his hard angles.

"It does feel good," she admitted. "Too good. Best you let me go."

He dropped his hands and released her, but she didn't move. He groaned, agonized. "Not fair."

"All the power, remember?"

"I remember," he said, aching. "How could I forget?"

She pulled away and took a few steps back. "What time do your folks arrive in town tomorrow?"

"After three," he replied.

"They should come for dinner. It would be good for Maisy to catch up in these surroundings rather than the hotel."

He agreed wholeheartedly. "They'll also be at the fair on Saturday. Maisy has agreed to be their tour guide."

"Wow," she replied. "I'm impressed."

"Me, too. By the way, where's your truck? I didn't hear you get home today."

"It's getting towed," she explained. "Broke down again right outside O'Sullivans Hotel."

"Bet they were happy about that."

"Oh, Liam's not such a grouch these days now that he's married to my friend Kayla."

Cole laughed. He knew about her friends. They'd talked a lot in the last couple of days. Every evening she came to the cabin and they sat on the small porch, drinking coffee or soda, chatting about anything and everything. And in those moments he felt as though they were the only two people on the planet. He learned that three of her closest girlfriends had all found love and married recently and she didn't see them as much as she used to. There was no envy in her words, she was just sort of melancholy. She talked about her father and stepdad, and sometimes she would say things about Pete, too. He listened without comment, trying desperately to ignore how it made him feel to know she'd loved someone once and clearly was too afraid to let herself feel that way again. And she spoke about the town and her work and every time they talked, every time he got to hear her soft voice speaking of things that were so important to her, Cole felt himself getting in deeper. And falling. Hard.

"I'll look at the truck when it gets here," he said.

She smiled in the sweet way he was becoming so used

to. "Thanks. I promised Maisy I'd watch a movie with her tonight. *The Notebook*," she added and grinned. "Want to join us?"

Cole grimaced. "I'd rather walk over broken glass... barefoot."

She laughed. "You might surprise yourself and enjoy the romance of it all."

"I can be romantic," he assured her, itching to haul her into his arms and kiss her sassy mouth. "Want to try me?" He looked up to the loft. "If only we had a balcony in here."

She laughed again. "Yeah, yeah, very funny, Romeo."

"You don't believe me?"

Her mouth twisted. "Do I believe that you can be romantic? Maybe. With an agenda."

He tapped his hand to his chest playfully. "An agenda? Do you think I'd resort to romantic nonsense to get what I want? I'm crushed."

"I'm sure you'll survive," she replied, smiling as she lifted the tarp a fraction. "Now, about this cart. I'm curious as to its—"

"Do you trust me?" he asked a little more seriously as he grabbed her hand. "Do you trust that I would never knowingly put your child in danger?"

She nodded, biting her lower lip. "Yes."

Cole raised her hand to his mouth and kissed her knuckles briefly. "Good. Jaye is going to be quite safe, I promise you. If I believed this race was beyond his capabilities, I'd say so. He'll be fine," he assured her. "And he wants you to see his cart for the first time on Saturday, at the starting line."

"Okay."

He smiled. "What? No argument? No resistance?"

"When I'm this close to you," she said huskily. "I'm really all out of resistance."

He wanted to kiss her so much in that moment that it took every ounce of his self-control to drop her hand and let her go. "You really need to get out of here."

"I know," she said and stepped back. "And, Cole, thank you for doing this with Jaye. I know it means the world to him."

"It means a lot to me, too."

He watched her walk away.

Wanting her so much he ached.

Ash liked Cole's family from the moment they climbed out of their rental car and greeted her on Friday afternoon. His dad, Ian, was bold and blustery and had the curliest auburn hair she'd ever seen. His mother, Zara, was stunningly beautiful, as were his two younger sisters, Scarlett and Aisha. And they loved him. The familial closeness was undeniable. And lovely to watch. They clearly loved Maisy, too, and Ash was delighted that the teenager was pleasant and welcoming to her grandparents and aunts over dinner. The house felt so alive and warm with everyone in it. Nancy played hostess brilliantly, while Uncle Ted regaled them with some of his navy tales and Jaye kept monopolizing Ian with talk about racing and his supersonic cart. Through all the talk, all the stories and all the laughter, Ash felt Cole's leg pressed against hers beneath the table. She liked the feeling. And wanted it, even if she wasn't quite sure why. She knew it was foolish. Knew she was asking for trouble. But the connection somehow felt like a lifeline. Something they both needed in the midst of their families getting to know one another.

Once dinner was over and dessert was ready to be served, Ash found herself in the kitchen with Zara and Cole's sisters, and handled their curiosity about the ranch and her career and the many children she fostered.

"Maisy is glowing," Zara said and smiled. "My son tells me that's all because of you."

Ash shrugged lightly and pulled the lemon meringue from the refrigerator. "It's not all my doing. He's worked hard on their relationship and he's being modest about it."

Scarlett laughed loudly "One thing my brother *isn't*, and that's modest."

"Hey," Cole said from the doorway, his lean frame leaning against the jamb, arms crossed, looking like the most gorgeous thing on two legs in worn jeans and a white shirt. "Stop ruining my reputation, sis."

Then there were several minutes of sibling badgering and insults that were said with such affection that Ash couldn't help but smile and envy the camaraderie he had with his sisters. They clearly all adored one another and it pleased her knowing that Maisy was part of such a loyal, loving family.

Later, once dessert and coffee was done and Micah and Tahlia had gone to bed, Jaye insisted on showing Cole's father his cart and all the males headed to the barn. His sisters and Nancy remained in the living room, looking over all the pictures on the mantel that depicted so many of the kids that had come and gone over the years, while Ash stayed on the front porch with Zara.

"It's such a peaceful place," the older woman commented. "Cole says you've lived here all your life?"

"Yes," Ash replied and wrapped her hands around the banister. "It's very special to me."

"I can see why," Zara replied. "I can also see why my son has become so attached to it."

She stilled. "Has he?"

His mother came to stand beside her. "I think so. And he doesn't get attached to things easily."

Ash suspected they weren't really talking about the ranch. "Mrs. Quartermaine, I'm not sure what you—"

"He's always been too devilishly handsome for his own good," she said and smiled. "And charming. And smart about things. Like women. Except for that viper he married. I never understood why he got involved with Valerie."

"Perhaps he thought it was time he settled down," Ash offered as heat rose up her neck. She really didn't want to have a conversation about his *ex-wife* with his *mother*. "You know, after the accident. Sometimes when a person is faced with their own mortality, it can make them think about the future."

"Cole talked to you about that?" Zara's expression softened. "I see. Well, he obviously trusts you. And you've done such a marvelous job with my granddaughter, I'm not sure we could ever repay you."

"Seeing Maisy happy, seeing her and Cole getting along—that's all the payment I need."

Zara patted her arm. "My granddaughter is lucky to have you in her life. So is my son."

Later, once the Quartermaines had returned to town and everyone else had turned in for the night, Ash sat by the window in her bedroom, looking out into the darkness, and she thought about Zara's words. Because she wasn't in Cole's life. She was on the edge. And only temporarily. He would be leaving soon and going back to his real life. And as she climbed into bed and turned off the light, Ash was stunned to realize how wretchedly unhappy that made her feel.

When she dragged herself out of bed the following morning it was past seven o'clock. She was tired and grumpy and since she'd spent most of the night awake and staring at the ceiling, she figured she needed another few hours' sleep to be fully functional. She knew Jaye would be jumping out of his skin over the race and when she reached the kitchen for a much-needed cup of coffee, he was already at the counter, shoveling cereal into his mouth under Nancy's watchful eye.

"Grandma said I gotta eat before I race," he said, wiping away some milk off his chin.

"She's right," Ash said and winked at her mother. "What time are you heading off this morning?"

"The race starts at eleven, but we gotta be there by ten o'clock to sign in," he said, his face beaming. "First we gotta make sure the cart is ready. Uncle Ted is coming, too, but Cole is driving us there, 'cuz he has to strap my cart down in the back of the truck. And Grandma is bringing Tahlia and Micah later. And I think Maisy is going with her grandparents."

It looked as though everyone had a plan for the day. The spring fair was an annual event and brought families and friends together from around the county. Ash had volunteered to help on one of the craft stalls for a couple of hours, but promised her son they would spend time together and that she would be there for the big race. It occurred to her, as he finished his breakfast and pulled on a sweater and cap, that he was more interested in getting the day started with Cole than hanging out with her. And she hated that it irked her. Jaye was growing up…and fast. He didn't need her like he once had. And today, as he raced out the door as quickly as his brace would allow, he clearly didn't need her at all.

Cole emerged through the back door about ten minutes later, informing her that he and Uncle Ted and Jaye were leaving. He looked so damned good she had to bite back a surge of resentment.

"So, I'll see you in a couple of hours?" he asked, hovering in the doorway.

She finished her coffee and managed a tight, forced smile. "Sure. Have fun."

He frowned, clearly picking up on her mood. "Everything okay?"

"Just fine," she replied stiffly. "I'll see you soon."

He lingered for a moment and looked as though he intended to say something. But he didn't, and once he disappeared, Ash let out a long breath, irritated and confused by her feelings.

"Are you two sleeping together?"

Her mother's voice got her attention immediately. She looked at Nancy, saw that her mother was regarding her with both brows raised curiously, and scowled. "Of course not."

"Well, maybe you should be," her mother said bluntly. "A few hours between the sheets with him might be exactly what you need to stop looking so...tense."

"Mom!" she admonished, mortified. "Really. What a thing to say."

"Oh, stop being such a prude, darling," Nancy said and chuckled as she waved a dismissive hand. "You've got eyes. And so have I," she said, brows up. "I've noticed the way he looks at you. And the way you look at him. Do something crazy for once in your life."

"I don't do crazy," she reminded her parent. "I'm too sensible."

"Too scared, more like." Nancy hugged her briefly. "Don't forget to live a little amid all that good sense."

The problem was, she knew what living a little meant. It meant feeling. It meant being seen. Being vulnerable. And the very idea of that petrified her through to her bones.

* * *

"Tell me," Nicola said to her a couple of hours later. "Why did we volunteer for this again?"

The small pedestal umbrella offered very little shade from the sun and Ash knew she'd made a mistake wearing the short green dress with narrow straps and a belted waist. Her shoulders were bare and already tinged pink from the midmorning sun. Nicola, with her olive skin and Italian heritage, didn't have to worry about burning as quickly, but even she was looking a little flushed.

"Because we care about our community and we were needed to help sell these crafts," she replied, sorting through the array of knitted teapot warmers and crocheted tea towels on the long table.

Nicola wrinkled her nose. "I'm so bored."

"Me, too," Ash admitted, waving a greeting to a few people she knew who wandered past. "But it's for charity."

"I'm obviously a bad person," her friend said and laughed. "Because I'm not feeling all that charitable right now. I've got so much work to do at the restaurant. And Marco and Johnny have been—"

"Do you think sex really relieves tension?" Ash asked and laughed, cutting off Nicola's complaining. "Or is it just a myth?"

Nicola stared at her. "You're asking *me* that? Me, who hasn't been on a real date in over a year." She shrugged and then chuckled. "I've almost forgotten what a date is. And sex."

Ash grinned. "You do know that Kieran is coming back to town for Kayla and Liam's wedding next month?"

Kieran O'Sullivan was Nicola's high-school boy-friend. The relationship had ended a long time ago—and ended badly—but Ash liked Kieran. He was her favorite O'Sullivan. They'd gone to school together and now he was a doctor in Sioux Falls. But with her friend Kayla and husband, Liam, renewing their wedding vows in a month, she knew he'd be there to stand in as best man for his brother. And she suspected Nicola was not entirely over her high-school sweetheart.

Nicola waved a dismissive hand. "Ancient history. I approve of Cole, by the way," she said and grinned as she changed the subject. "He's kind of the whole package—handsome, rich, funny...great with kids."

Ash ground her teeth together. Yes, he *was* perfect. She'd spoken to him several times that morning, each time with her *über*-excited son at his side. The patience and kindness he showed toward Jaye, toward everyone, made her fall for him more and more. She didn't like how it made her feel. Angry at herself, for starters. And she experienced a budding resentment toward him she would never have imagined she was capable of feeling. It lingered on the edge of her consciousness, drifting in and out each time he brought Jaye to visit her at the craft stand. Micah and Tahlia spent some time with him, too, and Maisy was coming and going with her family in tow. Except for Ian, who'd decided to find a shady spot under a tree and hang out with Uncle Ted.

"There's nothing going on between us," she stated, retidying the tidy piles on the table.

"Not yet," Nicola teased.

"He's leaving in a week," she reminded her friend.

"Seven long days and nights..."

Ash ignored the other woman's words, checked her watch, saw that it was close to eleven. "I have to go," she said and moved around the table. "Jaye's race starts soon."

Nicola waved a hand. "Wish him good luck from me."

Ash nodded and headed off to the other side of the fair. There were rows of stalls selling everything from jams to leather goods, face painting for the kids, pony rides and a huge inflated castle. There was wood chopping and a tractor pull and later that evening there would be a rodeo and fireworks display. Ash stopped to speak with a couple of officers on duty and then made her way past the rodeo grounds and to the grassy hill beyond that was teeming with people—race competitors, officials and supporters. Aside from the rodeo, the soapbox races were a major draw to the fair. Each race was age-appropriate and there were up to six competitors in each race to avoid congestion and maintain safety standards. Ash had to maneuver through the crowds to find the starting line, and her son.

When she did her heart almost burst inside her ribs. He was standing by his cart, chest puffed out, both Cole and Uncle Ted at his side. Ash approached and moved up behind him, placing her hands on his shoulders.

"Mom!" he said and turned, his face beaming proudly. "What do you think?"

She looked at the cart and smiled. It was meticulously put together, like a miniature race car, decorated in bright colors and pictures she knew were significant to her son. A child's drawing of the ranch house, the dogs playing in the yard, a police badge on the front and kids' smiling faces, one for every child that had come through their life over the years.

Pride washed over her and she marveled at the human being she had created. Her son was special, without a doubt. Ash looked at Cole, saw that he was watching her and managed a tight, wrenching smile.

"It looks amazing," she said. "You did a great job."

"Cole did most of the work," Jaye admitted and Ash's heart rolled over when Cole ruffled her son's hair affectionately. "But I did the decorating."

"It was a joint effort," Cole said and checked his watch.

"You're up in two minutes, kiddo, better get your safety helmet on and climb in."

"Will you be waiting for me at the bottom of the hill?" he asked, looking up at the man in front of him as though he was his own private superhero.

"You bet," Cole replied. "And remember, do it just like you did in practice. Go steady, go straight," he said and grinned. "Go hard."

Jaye looked around to the other competitors and Ash saw the slight tremble in his shoulders.

"What if I lose?" he asked, his confidence suddenly seeming to wane. "What if I come last?"

Ash was about to speak when Cole crouched down in front of him and placed the helmet in her son's hands. "Did I ever tell you about the time I raced and finished last? I'd won a race two weeks earlier and got all cocky and was convinced I'd win again. But I didn't. I blew it. I made a couple of bad decisions and ended up at the back end of the pack. And it sucked…big-time. But I didn't let it stop me from getting back on the track." He patted Jaye's shoulder. "And you won't, either. If you give it your best shot today, if you try your very hardest and still lose, then at least you lose with no excuses. And that's all that competing is about…trying your best."

Jaye's spirits seemed to pick up instantly. "Thanks, Cole. I'm gonna do that."

Cole nodded. "Then you've already won, buddy."

Ash fought the heat clawing at her throat and then hugged her son lovingly. "Good luck."

She stepped back and watched as Cole helped Jaye into the cart and he took his place alongside the other competitors. Ash snapped several pictures on her cell phone and then headed down to the bottom of the hill, so she could capture the moment her son crossed the finish line. She saw her mother in the bleachers with Micah and Tahlia and waved, then spotted Maisy and the rest of the Quartermaines sitting behind them. It touched her deeply to think how much support her son had in the crowd and as she continued her way down the hill, her eyes were hot and aching. She was the one who usually supported other people's children—to feel that reciprocated was a little overwhelming.

She found a spot at the bottom of the long hill, safely out of harm's way and behind a stack of straw bales that had been put into position to deflect any carts that were out of control. There were half a dozen other parents milling around the same area, all positioned in strategic spots for each child who was racing. She noticed that Cole had already made his way down the hill and was waiting at the end of the strip, a lanyard around his neck, indicating that he was Jaye's support crew. She noticed a couple of people pointing and talking and realized he had been recognized. But it didn't faze him at all. He was concentrating on Jaye and no one else.

A racing pistol fired, the crowd cheered and Ash's attention was solely focused on her child as he raced down the hill, his cart bobbing and weaving as he tried to keep it straight and fast. It was over quickly. Too quickly. And when all the carts finally came to a halt at the bottom of the hill she heard laughter and cheers and watched, mesmerized, as Jaye pumped his fists in the air. Cole was by the cart in a microsecond and Jaye was quickly out of the seat, balancing on his brace, his helmet off and his red hair plastered to his head. Just as Ash was about to race forward to congratulate her son, she saw him rush toward Cole. She stilled, unable to move as Cole laughed, lifted Jaye gently under his arms and swung him around.

Exclusion, raw and painful, filled her heart, her limbs and her whole body.

Jaye was laughing. Joyous. Overwhelmed. Happier than she had ever seen him before. When his feet were back on the ground he was still laughing, still pumping his arms in the air in a kind of gangly victory dance, still not noticing that she was barely four feet away.

"Did you see me!" he said to Cole, barely able to contain his excitement. "I came third! Third! How awesome is that."

Cole patted his back. "You did great. You kept it steady and straight."

"And fast," Jaye said with unbridled exuberance. "The third fastest!"

"I'm really proud of you, kid," Cole said. "You're the best."

Jaye looked at Cole as though he had just handed him the moon and Ash's insides ached even more. And in that moment she realized that her child, the child she had carried in her womb, the child she had brought into the world, the child she had nurtured and loved and protected all his life, had just been given something he desperately longed for. Something that made him feel whole and cherished and worthy. Something she had never been able to give him. Could never give him.

A father's pride.

"Look," Cole said. "Your mom's here."

She met Cole's gaze, their eyes locking as though by a magnetic force. She tried to smile, tried not to let her feelings of exclusion show, and hugged her son closely, inhaling the scent of his shampoo and loving him so much her insides ached. She couldn't breathe. Couldn't think. Couldn't do anything but feel helpless. And then foolishly resentful.

"You were incredible. Amazing," she said and hugged Jaye tightly.

"I'm gonna get a trophy," he said, beaming.

She knew how important that was to her son, knew he'd longed for a trophy to put on the mantel that was for something other than a math competition or chess tournament. Something athletic. Something where he wasn't defined by his leg brace.

Something she'd failed to give her son.

She'd protected him, kept him apart from anything she considered unsafe. Stifling him, she realized. Making him doubt himself, making him believe he had limits, boundaries.

She looked at Cole, saw him watching her with burning intensity, and knew he saw the hurt in her eyes. She muttered something about getting back to the craft stand for a while, but promised to return for the trophy presentation. Then she hugged her son once more before she turned and fled, never feeling more like a failure as a parent than she did in that moment. And she wanted to hate Cole for making her feel that way.

But instead, she could only love him for giving her child what she couldn't.

Chapter Nine

Cole was loading the cart onto the bed of Ted's old truck later that afternoon when he learned that Ash had left the fair and gone home early because she wasn't feeling well. Maisy informed him, and she'd been told by Nancy, who had taken charge of all the kids and was getting ready to take them for ice cream. His parents and sisters were hovering, too, full of praise for Jaye and his achievements. The boy held his trophy as though it was attached to his hand, and Cole remembered how Ash had looked when Jaye had been presented with his prize—incredibly proud... and something else. Certainly not ill, just sort of...sad.

It concerned him. A lot. Too much, because it was all he could think about as the afternoon dragged on. After the awards were handed out, Cole spent some time with his family over lunch and made small talk. Maisy was in good spirits and appeared to make an effort to get along with everyone—him included—and Cole was grateful for the opportunity to hang out with them all.

But by three o'clock he was driving back to the ranch in Ted's truck...alone.

He pulled up outside the barn and got out of the pickup. The two dogs came up and rushed around his legs and Cole gave them a pat in turn, while Rodney was walking up and down in his pen and the goats were bleating their customary chorus. Other than that, the place was quiet. Her old truck was parked beside the house so he knew she was home. Cole walked up the steps and tapped on the front door. Nothing. After a moment, he opened the door and entered.

He found Ash in the living room, sitting on a chintz love seat by the window, her legs crossed, her arms folded. Cole took a few steps into the room and stood behind the sofa. She looked so alone in the huge chair and he rested his hands on the back of the sofa, watching her, wondering what she was thinking behind her bright green eyes.

"Maisy said you weren't feeling well," he said quietly. "Are you okay now?"

She nodded, saying nothing.

"The kids are staying with your mom and Ted to watch the fireworks tonight."

Still nothing. Not a movement. Not a flicker.

"Ash...talk to me," he implored, feeling the pain in her drawn, unhappy expression through to his bones. Something was seriously wrong. "Please, say something."

She swallowed hard. She still wore the green dress, but her copper hair now waved around her shoulders. Cole's skin itched with the need to stride across the room and take her in his arms. But he stayed where he was, watching in silence as she got to her feet and walked toward the fireplace. She looked at the photographs for a moment, saying nothing, simply staring at the snapshots. Finally, she swiveled on her heels and met his gaze. Her eyes were bright, glittering like buffed emeralds.

"I've always believed I was good parent," she said, her voice shaky as she placed a hand to her chest. "I felt it in here. I never questioned it, never second-guessed myself. Maybe because I had to make all the decisions since the day Pete walked out." She made a brittle, almost scoffing sound. "Who am I kidding? Even when he was around he was close to useless in the parenting department. Still, I always thought that my son had everything he needed— all the love, all the support."

She stopped speaking for a moment and wrapped her arms around herself. When she spoke again the tears in her eyes were agonizing to see.

"But I was wrong," she said quietly.

"Wrong?" he asked. "How?"

"Because I haven't given him everything he needs." She shook her head. "Because I can't, and I can't because I'm his mother…his *mom*. That's my job. My role in his life. And it doesn't matter how good I am at it, how devoted I am, or how much I love him…it will never be all he needs."

The pain in her voice was unmistakable and he instinctively refuted her claim. "Of course it is, Ash. You've done an incredible job with him," Cole said gently. "He's such a great kid. He's amazing. He's smart and kind and funny— and he's all those things because of you."

Her lip trembled. "I know how special he is. And I've tried to raise him to be honest and respectful and kind to others. He's had it tough, too. Not just with the accident and the operations and the ongoing physical therapy, but with the way things are here on the ranch. With how he's had to share this place and his family with so many other children over the years. And he's never complained," she said and took a long breath. "Not once. And because he didn't complain, I thought he was getting enough, that he had all he needed. But I was so wrong."

"Ash, I don't think—"

"I've seen my son happy and sad and willful and stubborn and so many other things. But today... Today I saw my child experience something else—real joy," she said quietly, almost as though the word pained her. "I saw him so happy, so fulfilled, so proud of what he had achieved. And I know he felt that way because he had something today that he's never really had before—he had *you*."

Cole stilled and stared at her, not sure what he should say. He knew Jaye had become attached to him and Cole had come to care for her son in return. It was clear the kid was craving male attention—a father figure...a *dad*. And responsibility quickly pressed down between his shoulders. He felt guilty that he'd developed a relationship with her son and now she was hurting because of it. And guilty because he was leaving in a week and he suspected Jaye would feel as though he'd been abandoned. He'd become too involved, too quickly, and the young boy was going to pay the price.

"I didn't..." His words trailed off for a moment and he swallowed hard. "I didn't mean to make Jaye believe that my being here was, you know, permanent."

Her green eyes glittered brilliantly. "I know that. But he's come to worship you and I can't bear to think about how hurt he's going to be when you leave."

"I'm sorry," he said on a heavy breath. "I should have realized where this was heading a couple of weeks ago. But he was so excited about the soapbox cart and the race, I couldn't have refused to help him. He's such a great kid, Ash, and a credit to you."

She managed a tight smile. "I never realized how much

he missed having a man in his life. Someone who would listen to him and praise him and just be there. Someone he could look up to and learn from and hang off every word. Uncle Ted just didn't cut it, you know," she said tightly. "And then you arrived and he was besotted from day one. Not surprising, of course. In Jaye's eyes you're this *picture-perfect* image of what a father should be— strong, kind, considerate, trustworthy…you're everything that my son longs for. And there was a moment earlier today when I was so angry, when I resented you for being this *dadlike* figure that he's clearly wanted, but I've never given him. And I felt like such a failure as a parent. And then a fraud," she said and made a soft, self-deprecating scoffing sound. "Because you came to the ranch for my help, for my advice and guidance, and I feel as though the tables have been turned and I'm the one who needs help— I'm the one whose child is in trouble."

"Does it really matter?" Cole said quietly. "If we both needed help, then this all came about at the right time."

She shrugged. "I've never considered myself to be the kind of parent who needs help. But today, I realized that I've been so busy and so wrapped up in being a good police officer and a good parent and looking after foster kids and this ranch, I didn't take the time to let anyone into my life. Because I forgot that my life isn't only about *me*." She shook her head. "Or maybe I've known it all along, maybe I'm just terrified of letting someone in."

"That's understandable," he said quietly. "Considering."

"Because of my abandonment issues?" She gave a husky, brittle laugh. "Because my father and stepdad both walked out. Or since Pete broke my heart when he bailed on me and his son. I've talked about that very thing to countless kids over the years. I guess I should have had the same conversation with myself. But the idea that my child has been suffering because I've been too afraid to—"

Cole was around the sofa and reached her in a couple of strides. "You're gutsy and strong and not afraid of anything," he said, cutting her off as he grasped her hand.

She didn't pull away. She didn't move. Their gazes met, and linked, and Cole was quickly drawn deep into a connection that rocked him through to his blood and bones. His desire for her was intense and filled every part of him.

"I *am* afraid," she admitted, her voice quivering as she glanced to where their hands were linked together. "I'm absolutely terrified. Of you. Of…this."

"Me, too," he said quietly. "This thing between us, it goes both ways."

She nodded slightly. "So…what do we do?"

Cole shrugged. "I don't know. Ignore it. Go with it. Honestly, I have no idea how to compartmentalize how much I want you, Ash. It's kind of surreal and yet, unbelievably authentic."

The admission came out raw and honest. Like his uncontrollable desire for her. Like his growing *feelings* for her. And Cole knew she was as torn and confused as he was.

"You're leaving in a week."

"I know."

"And long distance is—"

"Impossible," he said, finishing her sentence as he gently rubbed her palm with his thumb. The action was hypnotic and sexy and she swayed toward him. "Ash…" He groaned out her name. "You'd better tell me to get out of here."

She reached up and touched his face, cradling his jaw, her fingertips electric against his skin. In all his life, he'd never had such intense chemistry with someone. He'd never felt as though he was at the mercy of his desire. But with Ash, he was all out of control.

"I should…" she said, her words trailing. "But somehow…I can't."

Cole swallowed, his throat tightening. "I promised myself, I promised *you*, that I would keep my distance and—"

"You said it was my decision," she said, cutting off his protests. "My choice."

"It is."

She traced his jawline softly. "So, this is my decision. My choice. I need to be with you, even if it's just for a moment, or an hour, or a day…" She sighed heavily. "Or a week."

Cole reached around her waist and tugged her close. She felt so good against him. So right. But he had to be certain. "Are you sure?"

She nodded. "I know what I want. And who."

He kissed her then, deeply and slowly, taking his time to move his mouth across hers, feeling her sigh as her lips parted and she let him inside. He went in, rolling her tongue around his as his hands moved to her hips and drew her harder against him. He kissed her again and again, anchoring her head gently as each kiss deepened. Finally, out of breath, Cole lifted his head and stared into her upturned face.

"We should probably take this somewhere else," he suggested. "The cabin?"

Ash shook her head. "Upstairs."

She grabbed his hand and led him upstairs and into her bedroom. It was a pretty, feminine room, decorated in pale cream and lilac, with a mountain of cushions on the bed and a purple duvet. The drapes were drawn and when she flicked on the bedside lamp the room lit up intimately. She closed the door and turned the lock, flipping off her shoes almost immediately. Cole stayed where he was by the end of the bed, his legs suddenly lodged in cement. She looked achingly beautiful in her dress and with her hair flowing around her shoulders.

"I haven't done this for a while," she admitted.

Cole took a couple of steps and reached for her hand. He rubbed her fingers and then brought her knuckles to his mouth and kissed them softly. "Is it stupidly macho of me to admit that I'm kind of happy about that?"

"Probably."

He chuckled and kissed her, pushing the strap of her sundress and bra off her shoulder to expose her creamy skin. Cole trailed his mouth down her jaw and neck and she turned her head, offering him greater access to her throat and the sensitive spot below her earlobe. He kissed her there, heard her moan in an encouraging way, and found the zipper on her dress, pushing it down with as much finesse as he could manage. Finally, the dress slipped off and landed at her feet, leaving her standing in a white lace bra and modest, high-cut briefs that were just about the sexiest things he'd ever seen.

"You're so beautiful you take my breath away," he said hoarsely.

And it was true. He did feel breathless. And humbled by her simple beauty and riveting colors—her bright copper hair, pink lips, pale skin lightly dusted with freckles. The very image of her almost brought him to his knees. He watched, mesmerized, as she twisted her hands behind her back and unhooked her bra. The garment fell away and he sucked in a sharp breath. Her breasts were fuller than he'd dare allow himself to imagine, her nipples rosy against the pale skin. She continued to undress, hitching her briefs over her hips and then down to her ankles. She stepped out of them and the dress, and moved closer.

Naked, she was pure temptation, torturing him more with each passing second. Cole stared at her, his appraisal long and deliberate, missing nothing. He silently pledged his intent to make love to her as thoroughly as she would allow.

He withdrew a foil packet from his wallet and tossed it on the bed and then, without a word, Cole stripped out of his clothes, chucking off the shirt, his shoes, jeans and briefs swiftly, until he stood in front of her. She looked at him. He looked at her. Cole had seen plenty of women naked over the years, but no one had ever had the profound effect on him that Ash McCune did. And he realized that what he was feeling was more than attraction. More than desire. And that making love with her would be more than sex. Much more. He'd been in love before, but this felt different from that, too. As she reached out and touched his chest, as her fingertips connected with his bare skin, Cole sucked in a sharp breath, feeling the connection through to his blood, through to his very soul. And in that moment he knew he was a goner. Done for. Out of his mind in love with this woman he'd known for only two weeks. The words burned on the edge of his tongue as they swirled around in his head. He wanted them out between them—full disclosure—so she knew exactly how much being with her meant to him. As she tilted her head and met his gaze, he experienced a connection so intense it amplified every feeling he had for her.

And she was his. For the moment. For an hour.

And as he reached out and gently cupped her nape, Cole realized she was the one woman he wanted for the rest of his life.

Ash had never seen a more beautiful man. His chest was smooth, his biceps honed and well-defined. Even the scar on his rib cage and another on his hip didn't detract from the perfect symmetry and beauty of him. She stilled and took a shallow breath. His arousal was unmistakable and she experienced a heavy feeling way down in her belly, feeling her body thrum with a kind of primal and instinctive desire she hadn't known she possessed.

The longing in his expression was like a narcotic and Ash was drawn toward him as he cupped the back of her neck, tilting her head gently. And then he kissed her, a long, sensually drugging kiss that was made even more erotic by the way their bodies were now pressed together, skin-to-skin, breasts-to-chest. His hands roamed down her back and anchored her hips, drawing her closer, making her want him more than she'd ever wanted any man, ever. And then they were on the bed, touching, stroking, discovering each other as one minute turned into two, and then five, and then ten, and longer. Time stilled, and suddenly the world didn't exist beyond the walls of her bedroom.

Ash had never experienced such rampant desire in all her life. He caressed and kissed her with a kind of instinctive confidence and it fueled her need to do the same. There was no hesitation in her touch, no reluctance to bare all that she wanted to give and receive in return. He worshipped her with his hands and mouth, trailing his lips down her collarbone and to her breasts. He took one straining nipple into his hot mouth and caressed the tender flesh with his tongue, until she was moaning his name over and over. He touched her intimately, his skillful hands drawing out her pleasure, making her writhe and press closer to his hard, lean body.

"Cole," she muttered against his throat, dragging her lips across the pulse that throbbed wildly in his neck. "Please... I want—I want..."

"I know," he said and then her words were smothered by

his kiss, his tongue dueling with hers in a dance that fueled her desire and need to have him above her, around her, inside her. She gripped him hard, returning each kiss, each touch, each erotic thrust of his tongue against her own and then she arched her spine in complete and utter surrender.

He grabbed the condom and, once it was in place, he moved over her, settling between her thighs. Ash relaxed, loving how the weight of him pressed erotically against her. She touched his flexing biceps as he supported himself on his elbows. And as he entered her slowly, he kissed her, over and over, his tongue mimicking the intimate way their bodies were joined.

"You feel so good," he whispered against her mouth.

Emotion burned behind her eyes and Ash marveled at the intense physical connection they shared. "So do you. This feels like—like…"

"Home," he moaned and kissed her deeply as he began to move, creating a silent, steady rhythm that catapulted her need for him skyward, driving her to place her hands on his back, urging him closer. And she matched every kiss, every gentle thrust, every soft word of encouragement until finally release claimed her and she let her body soar on a plateau of pleasure so torturously intense Ash thought she might pass out. And when he joined her, when his strong body arched and shuddered, she gripped him tightly, her growing love for him so overpowering in that moment that she couldn't hide the emotion in her heart and the tears in her eyes.

When it was over, he rolled over onto his back, his strong chest rising with each labored breath. He grabbed her hand, pressed her knuckles against his mouth and kissed her softly. After a moment, he excused himself and headed for the master bathroom. When he returned, he sat on the edge of the bed and reached for her hand again, holding it tightly within his.

"Everything okay?" he asked.

Ash nodded, surprised at her sudden lack of modesty. In the past she would have been pulling up sheets or looking for a robe. But she felt so comfortable around Cole, so at ease in his company, that even naked she was content to remain where she was. "I'm fine."

He wiped some moisture off her cheek with his thumb. "Tears?"

She shrugged lightly. "Not really. Just, you know…in the moment."

His grip on her hand tightened. "So, no regrets?"

Ash shook her head. "Not one. You?"

"No," he replied and traced a finger down her cheek and neck, lingering on the skin just below her collarbone. "And actually, I'm thinking we should do it again. And again," he said, moving lower. "And again."

She smiled and reached up, cradling his jaw. "You know what, I think you're right."

For the next two hours, they worked out ways to pleasure each other that went beyond anything she'd ever experienced before. And they talked, and then made love some more, and talked again. Afterward, once they'd showered, dressed and headed outside to feed and settle the animals in for the night, they returned to the kitchen for a snack. And as she moved around the room, doing things that were foolishly normal, Ash experienced a kind of happy lethargy that consumed her.

She made coffee and cut a generous slice from the apple pie in the refrigerator. Once they were at the table, sharing the pie and sipping coffee, she spoke. "It's getting dark. Once the fireworks are done everyone will come home."

He nodded and drank some coffee. "And life returns to normal, you mean?"

"Something like that," she said and shrugged. "This is all a little surreal."

"I suppose," he said and shrugged a little. "But at the same time, seems quite normal to me."

That was the strangeness of the situation. There was really no *morning-after* awkwardness between them. No regret. No guilt or hesitancy. Just a kind of easy companionship. She liked it. She liked him. She more than liked him.

She was, she knew, foolishly and crazily in love with Cole.

A man she hardly knew. A man who was leaving in a week.

"I didn't expect this to happen," she said quietly.

He met her gaze levelly. "I think making love was inevitable since the moment we met."

"That's not what I meant."

He swallowed hard and placed the mug on the table. "I guess that's where it gets complicated, when it feels like more than just a few hours of sex."

His admission warmed her through to the roots of her hair. And saddened her, too. Because it could never be. They had different lives and were separated by a thousand miles. There was no way around the inevitability of his departure and the knowledge she would probably never see him again.

"You know a long-distance relationship would never work," she said flatly. "I don't think either of us are cut out for one of those."

"Probably not. But, it might be worth a try."

She sat straight in the seat. "You…want to try?"

He half shrugged. "I don't want to wonder."

Ash stilled and looked down. "I need to think about it."

"Sure," he said softly. "We have time."

They had a week until he left. No time at all. "I don't think we should rush into anything."

"Chicken."

She met his gaze and saw that he was grinning. It made her laugh. And laughing made her feel foolishly warm and happy inside.

"That's better," he said and grasped her hand, turning over her palm and rubbing her skin with his thumb. "Don't be sad about anything that happened today, Ash. Your son had a great race and won a trophy. My parents got to spend time with Maisy and really connect with her. And you and I…" His words trailed off for a moment and he looked at her with riveting intensity. "You and I had an amazing afternoon."

"I'm not sad," she assured him. She pulled her hand away when she heard a vehicle pull up outside.

Her family was home. Ash got to her feet and quickly picked up the empty plate and her mug and walked around the counter. A minute later Jaye and Maisy raced into the room, followed by Micah and Tahlia, with her mother close behind. Her son immediately headed for Cole and began an excited chant about the race and winning his trophy and how it was the best day of his life. The younger kids had a drink of water and were then ushered off for bath time by Nancy, while Maisy came around behind the counter and rested her behind on the bench.

"Are you feeling better?" the teenager asked.

Ash managed a smile and nodded. "Much. Thank you. Did you have a good time with your grandparents and aunts?"

Maisy nodded. "They're pretty cool. It's a shame you guys missed the fireworks."

Ash glanced at Cole and noticed his jaw was set tight as he talked with Jaye, indicating he was aware of the conversation she was having with his daughter. "Maybe next year. But I'm glad you had a fun time."

Maisy shrugged, but Ash didn't miss the gleam of something else in her expression and for one mortifying moment wondered if the girl knew exactly what she and her father had been doing. When she dared meet Maisy's gaze again, Ash was quickly relieved. Maisy looked tired and ready for bed. "Yeah, well, I'm going to go to the cabin. See you later."

Ash watched as Cole got to his feet and moved toward the counter, his attention still focused on her son. By the time Jaye stopped speaking Maisy had already left. Jaye was still holding his trophy as though it was the most precious thing in the world and Cole continued to give her child his full attention. She loved that about him—loved that he made Jaye feel valuable and important and never disregarded him. She thought about how patient he'd been with Maisy. How he'd stepped up when she'd come into his life with hesitation. He was a good father, exactly the kind of role model a child needed. Exactly what *her* child needed.

She told Jaye to get ready for bath time and once he'd left the room, she met Cole's level gaze. "Thank you."

"For what?" he asked.

"You know, for Jaye—for making him a priority today."

"I care about him," Cole said quietly.

"I know that," she said and offered a tight smile. "It's very mutual. He's going to miss you when you're gone."

"It's very mutual," Cole said, echoing her words as he reached for her hand and pulled her close. "And I'm going to miss you, too," he admitted a little raggedly as he took a breath. "I'm going to miss you every minute I'm not this close to you during the next week."

Ash knees weakened. "Me, too. But you know, with the kids and my mom and everything that—"

"I know," he said, cutting her off. "But, perhaps we could do something together. Like a date."

"A date?"

"Yeah," he said and smiled. "Maybe you'll let me take you out for dinner to that fancy hotel in town. Jaye told me you like to dance," he said, urging her closer until she could feel the heat of his skin mesh with hers. "So, maybe dinner, conversation, a little dancing. Away from the curious eyes of your mom and our kids. And then before we get home we could make out for a while in the car."

Her weakened knees almost gave way. "Sounds like the perfect evening."

It did. But Ash knew it could never be. A date would be pointless. And it would only set her up for more heartbreak. "But I can't. I can't…risk myself, Cole. I've done that before and ended up in pieces." She pulled away. "I need to go and check on Jaye."

He nodded and released her. "Yes, I should spend some time with my daughter. I'll see you tomorrow."

Ash managed a shallow breath. Her heart pounded. Her legs were uncharacteristically wobbly. And part of her didn't want to say good-night. Part of her wanted the evening to go on and on and never end. She stepped back and felt the chasm of space between them so profoundly she ached inside. "Good night, Cole."

"'Night, Ash. Sweet dreams."

She watched him walk away, experienced a tug of longing so intense it almost made her call after him. But she didn't. It was time to remember that he was leaving in a week and she had to keep her heart and sanity intact for the sake of her family and the valuable life she'd led before Cole steamrolled into it.

It was time to end the fairy tale.

Chapter Ten

"This is a lovely place. And being here suits you."

Cole looked at his mother, saw a curious gleam in her eyes and decided to ignore it and the conversation he figured he was about to have. It was Maisy who had suggested a picnic by the river on Sunday afternoon, Maisy who rang his parents and invited them and coordinated the event with Nancy and Ash. His family was returning to Phoenix the following morning and had jumped at the chance to spend more time with their granddaughter. Of course, he was happy that Maisy had initiated the get-together and was clearly mellowing toward her newfound family. But he also felt unusually cloistered by the whole scene.

"It's a nice spot," he said and skipped a stone across the water. He'd been standing alone up until a few minutes earlier. After lunch, he'd wandered off by the water's edge, fueled by his thoughts and the need to be alone. "And good weather."

His mother laughed softly. "Oh, I see."

Cole frowned and glanced sideways as he crossed his arms. "You see?"

"We're at the talking-about-the-weather stage. So, you like it here."

He shrugged. "Sure. It's a nice spot, like I said."

"Caught between two worlds, huh?"

Cole let out an exasperated sigh. "What are you talking about, Mom?"

She stood beside him, elegant and intuitive and irritating. "I know how hard it was for you to give up racing. And I know you've been treading water ever since, trying to figure out what to do with your life. I know you married Valerie because you needed an anchor after you almost died in that crash. And I know that you want to be a good father to Maisy."

Cole's gut twitched. "Mom, I don't—"

"I also know that you're not truly happy managing the race team."

"I'm happy enough," he said quietly.

"That doesn't really cut it. And maybe you haven't even realized it yourself," she said and patted his arm. "But, I'm your mother and I can sense these things in my children. I know you want…more."

He shrugged uncomfortably. "Doesn't everyone?"

"Don't let geography or the issues of your past dictate your chance for happiness, that's all I'm saying."

"Mom, I'm not sure what you think is going on here, but I—"

"I think you've found something you've been looking for," she said, cutting him off. "I think you really care for this girl. And I think she really cares for you."

Cole ignored the heat smacking his cheeks. "And you've figured this all out over the course of one weekend?"

"I figured it out by spending two minutes in a room with the pair of you," she said bluntly. "I've been in love with your father for nearly forty years—I know what it looks like."

Cole sighed heavily. "It's…complicated."

"Then uncomplicate it," his mother said and smiled. "Tell her how you feel."

"I can't. Maisy needs me to—"

"Maisy needs you to be happy," she said and squeezed his arm again. "That's as simple as it gets, Cole. And if Ash makes you happy, if she's the one woman who can hold your heart, then let her know. What have you got to lose?"

Everything.

He didn't say it. He didn't want to think about his mother's words. There was no point. He was leaving in a week and Ash had made her feelings clear. She wouldn't risk herself, her life or her family on the chance that they could make something together.

Cole watched his mom walk back toward the group and saw how happy and connected everyone looked together. Uncle Ted and his father were tossing a baseball with the younger kids, Maisy and his sisters were standing around the picnic table with Ash and Nancy. And when his mother joined the group there was laughter and he was astounded when he saw his daughter allow Nancy to put a companionable arm over her shoulder. *Family.* The word jolted through him. The scene seemed crazily normal. As though they all belonged together. His gaze found Ash, laughing at something his mother said, her beautiful copper hair flowing around her shoulders, her green eyes wide and filled with happiness. He loved her laugh. And her hair. And the soft curves that fit so perfectly against him.

I love her.

Admitting it was cathartic.

And petrifying.

He didn't know what to do, maybe for the first time in his life. Cole sucked in a deep breath and walked toward the group. Ash had moved around to the other side of the table and was looking at him long before he reached her, her warm gaze like a homing beacon. He moved beside her and swiped a cookie from the container she was packing.

"Everything okay?" she asked, tapping his hand playfully.

"Fine," he replied and grabbed a soda from the cooler. "You?"

She nodded. "Great. Everyone seems to be having a good time. You have a really great family."

"You, too."

"Family is everything," she said softly and placed the used cutlery in a container. "Oh, I heard from Ricky this morning. He said that he's settling in well at his new school. He also said to say hello to you and Maisy."

"That's good news. So, will you be taking any more kids in the short term?"

She shrugged. "I'm not sure. Micah and Tahlia need a permanent placement, but until they're settled and hopefully adopted, I really don't want too much change around the ranch. And I think I need to spend some quality time with Jaye. He's going to miss you and Maisy when you leave."

He understood. He knew she was worried about her son's attachment to him and what it would mean for Jaye when he and Maisy left the ranch. "Ash, I think we need to—"

"Cole!"

Jaye's voice cut off his words and the boy moved between them. "What is it, buddy?"

"Can you show Uncle Ted how to throw a curveball?" he asked. "Your dad said you were a pitcher in high school."

Ash's brows came up. "Is there anything you can't do?"

Tell you I love you...

He shrugged and spoke over his shoulder as he walked away. "How about you make it your mission to find out."

She laughed and the lovely sound vibrated through his chest. He spent the following hour teaching Jaye and Micah how to pitch and by the time the afternoon wrapped up it was after three o'clock. Cole followed his family back into town and while he was at O'Sullivans, he made a dinner reservation for Wednesday evening. He hung around for an hour and then headed back to the ranch. Maisy was on the sofa in the cabin with a book in her hands when entered.

"Can I have a driving lesson in the morning?" she asked. "You promised," she reminded him and grinned.

"Sure," he replied. "If the schoolwork is done."

"I finished my geography paper," she said and nodded. "Warden."

Cole chuckled. "Parent," he amended.

Maisy's gaze dropped and she sighed. "I guess I don't make it easy sometimes."

"Sometimes?"

She looked up. "Okay...all the time."

"It's not your job to make mine easy."

"Um...I guess. So, when I get my license will you buy me a car?"

Cole rocked back on his heels. The question indicated the future. Their future...as a family. Cole felt as though he'd just been handed the moon. "I'll think about it."

"I could always drive one of yours."

His Jeep or treasured red Mustang? Not a chance. "Good try, kid. Feel like a game of Scrabble and burned burritos later?"

"You can't cook."

"I did say burned," he reminded her.

Maisy laughed. "Maybe I need to give you cooking lessons," she suggested. "We could trade them for driving lessons and then for the car you're going to buy me."

Cole's mouth curled. "My cooking isn't *that* bad."

She made a face. "It's the worst. You burn water."

He laughed and it felt good. "Okay...deal. So, how about this game of Scrabble?"

"Sure. I told Ash today how much I enjoy beating you at board games."

"Game on, kid," he said as he walked down the hall. "Game on."

And as he heard his daughter laughing, Cole realized he might just get the fathering thing right, after all.

Ash went back to work and by Tuesday had almost put out of her mind the crazy events of the weekend. Cole's family arriving en masse. The spring fair. Jaye's achievement in the soapbox race. The family picnic. And making love with Cole.

Which, of course, was the one thing her heart *and* traitorous libido wouldn't allow her to forget. Each time she saw him, each time he was within a six-foot radius, she was bombarded with memories and feelings.

Because a few of her colleagues were taken ill with the flu, she went out on patrol with one of the ordinance enforcement officers and when she returned it was after lunch. She was called into Hank's office around one o'clock and was startled to learn that the current sergeant was being transferred to another county and that she was in line for promotion if she wanted to apply. It meant more responsibility, a better salary and longer hours. Which is exactly what she said to her friend Nicola when she saw her that afternoon, stopping in at JoJo's before she headed home.

"But, do you want the job?" Nicola asked and pushed a latte across the counter to her.

"I'm not sure. I mean, I like the idea of it. However, the hours are longer and I would probably have to give up some of my volunteer work. And maybe I'll have to rethink how much fostering I do. I know my mom and Uncle Ted would be supportive, but I don't want anything to affect Jaye."

"Being a single mom is hard," Nicola said and sighed.

Ash nodded. "And we have a support network around us. I don't know how I'd cope if I didn't have my mom and uncle. Like Maisy's mother, who did it alone for over thirteen years. And through a terminal illness."

Nicola smiled sadly. "Poor Maisy. But, she's got her dad now, and that seems to be working out."

"Yes," Ash said and sighed. "She's coming around."

"And Cole?" Nicola asked. "How are things in that department?"

"He and Maisy have—"

"I meant between you and him," Nicola said, cutting her off.

"Oh, you know, sex always complicates things."

Nicola almost spat out her coffee. "Whoa, back up. You slept with him?"

Ash nodded. "Although technically, we didn't do a whole lot of *sleeping*."

Her friend's eyes bulged. "Are you in love with him?"

"I think so," she replied candidly.

"Is he in love with you?"

Ash sighed heavily, wondering about the question she'd asked herself countless times over the past three days. "I don't know. I mean, when we're together it's so easy and comfortable and yet, it's also intense and incredibly passionate. And when we're apart, I think about him and want to be with him, to talk to him and just listen to the sound of his voice. It's like we've known one another forever. And sometimes, I feel him watching me and think, yes, he feels this, too. But I'm not good at this stuff," she said, her throat tight with emotion. "After Pete, I closed down. I stopped feeling and concentrated on things that wouldn't break my heart. But with Cole, I feel vulnerable and achy and so out-of-my-league in the feelings department. The thing is, he's nothing like Pete. They're opposites in every way. Cole is strong and sensible and reliable and he really stepped up to be a father when he found out about Maisy. Whereas Pete..."

"Bailed the moment things got hard?" Nicola said, finishing her thought.

Ash shrugged. "Honestly, I think we were done way before then. If Jaye's accident hadn't happened, something else would have driven him off. It was all the excuse he needed to walk out. And with Cole, it's crazy to even think we could make it work. He lives a thousand miles away. He has a career. A life. A family. And so do I. For it to work, one of us would have to give up everything."

"And you couldn't?"

Ash shook her head. "My life is here. My son's life is here. And Cole needs to give Maisy a stable and secure home, surrounded by her grandparents and aunts. His family business is like a dynasty and he would never give that up and I couldn't ask him to. It's impossible to imagine it could be any other way."

Nicola nodded. "So, it's settled. It's not going to happen."

"Exactly. And I'm doing the right thing by making sure nothing else happens between us while he's here, don't you think?"

Nicola grinned. "You asking me for advice? The poster child for failed romantic relationships? I think you should do what feels right."

The problem with that, Ash thought as she left JoJo's and headed home, was that what *felt* right was impossible. Being in Cole's arms felt right. Watching him with her son felt right. Spending time with his daughter felt right. Imagining them as a family felt right.

When she arrived home it was nearly five o'clock and she spotted a brand-new silver pickup parked outside the barn. Jaye, Micah and Uncle Ted were circling the vehicle and when he saw her pull up, Jaye came over to her, hands waving excitedly.

"Mom, Mom! Isn't it awesome?"

Ash looked at the truck, with its sleek lines and shiny paint, and then at her uncle. "Nice rig. Who does it belong to?"

"You," Jaye announced and grinned. "Us! It's ours."

Ash stared at Ted and frowned. "What?"

"Joss Culhane dropped it off an hour ago," Ted explained. "Said he picked it up from Rapid City this morning. Said it belonged to you."

Confusion clawed up her neck. "That doesn't make sense. It's a mistake. Why one earth would——"

"I don't think it's me you should be asking about this," Ted said and waved a hand in the direction of the cabins.

Ash snapped her head around. Cole sat on the porch of his cabin, feet stretched out, wearing jeans and a white T-shirt. Heat climbed over her skin and she turned, instructing Jaye to stay with his uncle because she knew he would follow her otherwise. And with every step she got hotter and madder. When she reached the cabin, she halted by the bottom step and glared up at him, chest heaving. And he was smiling as he looked her over.

"By the expression on your face I guess I don't have to ask if you're responsible for this?" she said, hooking a thumb in the direction of the barn.

He shrugged.

"Don't do that," she said angrily. "Don't look all innocent and make out as though this isn't a big deal. Because it is a big deal. It's a *huge* deal."

He shrugged again. "It's just a truck."

"It's a brand-new, very expensive truck," she said, tapping her foot on the bottom step. "And it's not staying here. Send it back."

"The truck stays," he said and shook his head. "There's no point being stubborn about this."

Rage curdled through her blood. "I don't want it."

He cocked a brow. "What? You don't want a safe, reliable vehicle to transport your family around in? This reaction is simply your pride talking."

"It's not pride," she spluttered. "It's—it's…good sense. A vehicle like that is way out of my budget and I—"

"It's a gift," he said, cutting her off.

"It's excessive."

He shrugged again, infuriating her. "I can easily afford it, therefore it's not excessive."

"Can you hear yourself?" she demanded. "Maybe you think it's okay to live in a world where money solves everything, but I can't be bought."

He shot to his feet. "I'm not trying to buy you. I'm trying to *thank* you."

"I don't need—"

"Do you know where my daughter is right this minute?" he said, cutting her off again. "With your mom, making brownies. And today she asked me if we could get a cat when we get home. *Home*, Ash. She called my apartment her home. She's never done that before. For the past few days she's been talking about the future. About school and joining the drama society and going on a vacation with me and her grandparents. Things I never imagined she would say. And that's because of you. Because she's here, with you. Because of how you and your family have made her feel, I think she's actually healing."

Emotion clutched at Ash's throat and she swallowed hard. "I'm happy that Maisy has started accepting you, Cole, but buying a gift that extravagant is out of the question. I can't accept it."

He exhaled heavily and moved down the steps. "Is this because we made love?"

God, she was dying inside. She wanted to fall into his arms and forget every reason she shouldn't. "No...yes...I don't know. All I know is that I cannot accept such generosity. Not from anyone."

He held her gaze. "I didn't realize I was just anyone."

Ash closed her eyes for moment and took a long breath. "That's not what I meant. But things are complicated enough and—"

Cole grabbed her hand and placed a set of keys in her palm. "Keep the truck. Or sell it." He released her and stepped back. "If you can't accept it for yourself, then do it for your mom, or your uncle or your son. And I'd like to take you to dinner tomorrow night. Just you and me," he added. "No kids. No chaperones. A proper date."

He turned and headed up the steps and disappeared into the cabin before she had a chance to respond. Stunned, Ash remained where she was for a moment. She looked toward the truck and her son and uncle and then back toward the cabin. She finally found some energy to move her legs and walked to the main house. She found her mother and Maisy in the kitchen, baking up a storm. They both looked up when she entered the room, but it was Maisy who spoke first.

"You look mad," the teenager said and grinned. "He said you would be."

"He's right," she said stiffly, meeting her mother's curious gaze.

"It's a generous gift," Nancy said as she measured out cocoa powder.

"Too generous," Ash said as she dropped the keys on the table and sat down.

"You do know he's rich, right?" Maisy said, brows raised in an endearingly familiar way that was so much like her father it made Ash's insides ache. "Like, really rich? The whole family is."

"That's no excuse," Ash said stiffly, fighting her anger at him for being so high-handed and arrogant. "Money doesn't buy happiness."

"No," Maisy mused. "But it does buy shiny new trucks. And he won't take it back. He's stubborn."

Nancy chuckled. "You may as well admit defeat on this one, Ash."

She shook her head. "I can be stubborn, too."

Her mother gave a wry smile and said cryptically, "Make sure it's for the right reasons."

Ash managed a weary nod and headed upstairs. She showered and changed into cotton cargoes and a green T-shirt, ignoring the bed that reminded her way too much of Cole. She thought about his parting words. A date. The two of them. No kids. No chaperones.

Jerk.

There was no way she was going on a date with him. Not a chance.

Which is exactly what she told her mother the following morning once the kids had eaten breakfast and were getting ready for their homeschooling lessons.

"It is a little romantic," Nancy said and rinsed the coffee mugs. "And it wouldn't hurt you to embrace a little romance."

"And risk everything?"

"Everything?" Her mother's eyes widened. "Or just your guarded heart?"

"He's leaving on Saturday," Ash reminded her.

"A lot can happen in four days. He likes you. You like him," Nancy said and smiled. "Why don't you simply see where that takes you."

"Because it's pointless," she stated hotly. "It doesn't matter that I like him. It wouldn't matter if I was crazy in love with him—the outcome would be the same."

"Are you?" Nancy asked, brows up. "Crazy in love with him?"

"I don't do crazy," she said, her expression tight.

"Well, maybe it's time that you did," her mother suggested. "And you should wear the blue dress tonight—the one with the buttons up the front."

"I'm not going," she said, standing her ground.

But she did go. And she did wear the blue dress. He collected her at her door at six thirty, looking achingly gorgeous in pressed black trousers and a light gray shirt open at the collar. And he smelled so sexy she had to force herself not to inhale the scent that was uniquely his and had somehow become a narcotic for her senses.

"What exactly did you tell Maisy we were doing tonight?" she asked quietly, once they were in the rental car and driving from the house. "Did you tell her this was a date?"

"No," he replied. "But I'm not in the habit of sharing the details of my personal life with my daughter." He waited a moment and then spoke again. "I simply said we were going out and didn't elaborate."

"What if she suspects something?"

"Suspects what? That we're having dinner together? I'm pretty sure she won't care one way or another. It's dinner, Ash, not a weekend in Vegas."

Heat crawled up her neck. "So, this is simply dinner?"

"Of course. Isn't that how a first date usually goes?"

"Oh, this is a *first* date," she said *über*-sweetly. "Thanks for clearing that up."

He made an impatient sound as they crossed the bridge and headed into the center of town. "Is this about the truck?"

"What?"

"The truck," he repeated. "Are you still mad about that? I noticed you drove your old pickup to work this morning."

"Of course I did," she said tightly. "And of course I'm still mad at you. I'm not the kind of woman who is impressed by diamonds and private jets."

He laughed. "It's a truck, not an engagement ring."

Ash burned from the soles of her feet to the roots of her hair. "I wasn't suggesting… I mean, I didn't think for one minute that—that…"

He laughed again, louder this time as he turned the vehicle into the O'Sullivans Hotel parking lot and zipped into a space. "Lost for words? That's a first."

Ash got out and slammed the door. "You're such a jerk."

He met her around the passenger side. "You look beautiful, by the way. Nice dress."

She glared at him. "Good try. But it won't work. I'm immune to your charms."

His eyes glittered. "Really?" he said and grasped her arm gently, pulling her close. "Care to prove that theory?"

"Don't even think about kissing me," she said hotly.

He pressed closer and draped a hand on her hip. "I'm not going to kiss you. Unless you ask me to. Which you'll do in about ten seconds flat if I do this," he said and grasped her chin, tilting her head back slightly. "And this," he added, trailing his thumb along her jawline and then tracing her lower lip, and then her top lip, so excruciatingly slowly that the sensation made her arch involuntarily toward him. "Or maybe this," he said, moving his hand down her throat and grazing his knuckles across her skin.

"Cole," she said, and sighed. "Stop…please."

He chuckled softly. "Okay," he said and dropped his hand as he put space between them. "Let's go inside."

The main restaurant at O'Sullivans was well appointed and offered international cuisine. With starched white tablecloths, fine bone china, excellent service and the kind of menu found in big-city hotels. The place was busy, but Cole had obviously booked a table and they were seated quickly. He ordered wine without looking at the menu and once the waiter disappeared, he gave her a kind of sexy smile that made her knees tremble.

"Would you stop being so—so damned perfect," she said and sighed.

He grinned. "I do have my flaws."

"Name one?" she challenged.

"I can't sing," he replied. "And we've already established that I can't cook. And you did accuse me of being a lousy kisser a while back."

She smiled. "I think we both know that's not true. So, what else?"

"You want to hear about more of my flaws?" His mouth twisted. "I'm afraid of spiders."

"And?"

"And when I was fourteen I ate shellfish to get out of a history exam."

Ash's eyes bulged. "That could have killed you."

He shrugged and nodded. "Not my best decision. And not one I've repeated, since I spent three days in hospital. What about you?"

The waiter returned and once the wine was poured, Ash raised her glass and smiled. "I'm afraid of clowns. If I ever took Jaye to a kid's birthday party and they had a clown, I'd end up hyperventilating and hiding in the bathroom."

"Anything else you're afraid of?"

"Slasher movies. Rogue waves. Falling in love with you."

As the words left her mouth it was as though every sound around them disappeared. He stilled, but she saw the glass in his hand tilt unsteadily and a few drops of wine landed on the tablecloth.

He put down the glass and rested his hands on the table. "Well, I guess you can avoid the slasher movies. And I don't imagine you'll be experiencing a rogue wave in South Dakota anytime soon. As for the other thing," Cole said quietly, his gaze unwavering as he grabbed her hand and entwined their fingers intimately, "it's not something you should be afraid of."

"You don't know what you're saying…"

"I know exactly. I know what I'm feeling. And I hope it's what you're feeling, too."

Ash's throat closed over. "It's an impossible idea."

"What if it's not?" he said softly. "What if it's exactly the thing that's meant to happen? What if the reason I came here, the reason your cousin suggested it in the first place, was so that we could end up right here, right now?"

She couldn't breathe. Couldn't move. Couldn't do anything except stay trapped in the intensity of his gaze. And wish that things were different. Wish that they didn't live a thousand miles from one another. Wish that they didn't both have family they loved and obligations keeping them tied to the lives they had.

Ash found the courage to ask the question burning through her blood. "Are you saying that you're...in love with me?"

He stared at her. Long. Hard. And the moment seemed to stretch into eternity. Then he spoke. One word.

"Yes."

Chapter Eleven

If he'd been prepared for the question, if he'd known he was going to lay his heart on the line, Cole would have ensured he had a ring in his pocket and then dropped to his knee and asked her to marry him. But the tiny lick of good sense he had left screamed inside his head that it was too soon, and a busy restaurant where she was easily recognized wasn't the place. Then the waiter returned and they were suddenly perusing menus and ordering food. Once the waiter left their table he couldn't remember what selection he'd made. But the distraction had given Ash the opportunity to pull away and hold her hands in her lap.

He was burning to ask if she felt the same. But oddly, there seemed to be so much white noise around them, he wasn't sure he'd hear her response. It was as though a brass band was suddenly playing in his head, drowning out everything but the thunderous beat of his heart behind his ribs. And he realized she looked out of sorts. Uncomfortable. As though his admission was the last thing she wanted to hear.

"Are you okay?" he asked.

She nodded fractionally. "Sure."

"If you want to talk about it, we can."

She shook her head just as a woman—tall, blond and elegantly beautiful—approached their table. Ash introduced her as Kayla O'Sullivan and Cole remembered that this was the friend who was married to the owner of the hotel and who was expecting her first child. They made small talk for a few minutes, about the hotel and the weather, and he congratulated her on the impending birth. When she left he noticed that Ash was watching him and not her friend.

"What?"

"You're very charming."

He smiled and drank some wine. "I thought you were immune."

"Turns out, I'm not," she admitted. "And I'm not sure if that's bad luck, or good fortune."

"Shall we simply roll the dice and see where it takes us?"

She shook her head. "I can't be that cavalier. The kids…"

"Are more resilient than you think," he said quietly. "And Jaye and Maisy in particular. Look at what they've both been through in their short lives."

"Exactly," she said. "And I'm not going to make my son's life even more complicated by starting something that has no chance of working out."

"We've already started this," he reminded her. "We became friends. And then we kissed. And then we made love. And it was…incredible."

"It was," she agreed. "But it can't happen again. You came here to work on your relationship with Maisy and I'm not going to be the reason that gets derailed."

Cole understood her concerns. He had them, too. But he believed she was being overcautious. Kids got through things. Kids learned to accept new situations. And Cole didn't believe Jaye would have a problem with him dating his mom. Or more than that. As for Maisy, she was older and would be able to handle him being in a relationship. Cole was about to respond when their meals arrived. They ate in silence and once they had finished, Ash declined dessert or coffee.

"I'd like to go home now," she said and pushed her half-full glass of wine aside.

Cole checked his watch and saw that it was barely eight fifteen. "A little early, don't you think? We're on a date, remember? And I promised I'd take you dancing."

"I don't want to dance." She sighed heavily. "Please take me home."

Cole registered her unhappiness and nodded. "Okay, if that's what you want."

"It is."

Five minutes later the check was paid and they were back out by the curb. He opened the passenger door of the car and she got in wordlessly. The drive back to the ranch was done in heavy, uncomfortable silence. Cole walked her to her door, climbing the steps behind her. The sensor light flicked on and she reached for the knob.

"Ash, can we—"

"Thank you for dinner," she said, cutting him off. "Good night."

Cole expelled a heavy breath. "This conversation will still be here in the morning."

She shrugged lightly. "This conversation needs to be over. It's Wednesday—you're leaving on Saturday. That's three more days, Cole. What can we do in that time? Fall into bed again? Pretend that the end isn't inevitable? I know what people leaving feels like," she said, her voice filled with emotion. "And I don't want that again. I don't want to feel that with you. Because honestly, I don't think I'd survive it."

She headed inside and closed the door. Cole remained on the porch for a few minutes, tempted to knock on the door and talk to her some more. But he didn't. He walked back to the cabin, found that Maisy had already turned in for the night and was grateful he didn't have to answer any questions from his daughter about where he'd been. He'd told her he was going out with Ash and she'd merely shrugged and said "whatever" in that bored way of hers.

Cole took a shower, dropped into bed and stared at the ceiling for a few hours.

Thinking. Dwelling. Realizing that he'd just made a giant-sized horse's ass of himself.

He'd admitted his feelings for Ash and she'd closed up like a clam. It was too much, too soon, and something he'd never normally do. He'd been dating Valerie for nine months before he'd said the words to her, *and* they had been on the brink of moving in together. It wasn't a two-week acquaintance, a few kisses and one amazing afternoon in bed.

He had seriously screwed up.

And miscalculated the depth of their relationship.

It was past seven when he got up the following morning, and after having breakfast with Maisy she headed off to the main house for her lessons with Nancy and the other kids. Cole spent the rest of the morning cleaning up and then made a few telephone calls. He would be back at work the following week, back to all that was familiar. He had a race team to manage and had meetings scheduled in San Francisco and Dallas a couple of weeks out to discuss sponsorship for the next two seasons. A few days' home and he'd be back into the familiar rhythm of his life. Maisy would be back at school, he'd visit his parents every Sunday and maybe start dating someone new. Someone who at least lived in Phoenix. That was the future that seemed inevitable. And in some way, the idea left him feeling bereft and unhappy.

It was four o'clock that afternoon when he saw Ash again. He was in the barn, tinkering with an old tractor that hadn't worked for years, and she strode toward him, hands on hips, green eyes blazing. She looked as mad as hellfire.

"Where are the kids?" she demanded.

"Up at the house playing a video game under Ted's supervision," he replied.

She nodded slowly. "Good. And my mother?"

"At a charity meeting in town, something to do with the museum. She said she'd be back before dinner." His mouth twisted. "Something on your mind?"

She glared at him. "You had no right to say that to me last night," she said and stood a few feet from him, chest heaving.

"Say what?" Cole asked as he wiped his hands on an old towel. "That I was in love with you?" He shrugged lightly and rested his behind on the workbench. "It's the truth."

"Maybe. But now it's all I can think about," she admitted with a kind of anguish that made him ache inside. "And I can't have my head filled with this kind of thing. I have too many responsibilities. My family, this place, my job—I can't switch all that off and race into the sunset with you, Cole, no matter how much I might be tempted."

She looked so gorgeous in her uniform that he had to pull on all of his self-control to remain where he was and not stride across the barn and haul her into his arms. "Have you been stewing on this all day?"

"Of course I have," she said hotly. "Haven't you?"

He lifted one shoulder and was about to respond when she spoke again.

"And it ruined my day. Did I tell you that I got offered a promotion the other day?" she shot back irritably. "There's a sergeant position coming up and I'm in line for the job."

"Congratulations."

Her gaze narrowed. "Don't you see? It's just one more thing that makes *this* impossible." She gestured to the two of them.

Cole stared at her. She was being stubborn. Hard-headed. Impossible. And he wanted to kiss her so much that his entire body tingled. But he had to make her see that sometimes caution wasn't the sensible option...that sometimes the prize was worth the risk.

"Ash, I've learned to believe that anything is possible. If I didn't challenge that ideal I probably wouldn't be on my feet right now."

Ash's skin burned. The sound of his voice was like a narcotic, feeding her addiction for him with every word. But she had to show good sense. She had to keep her wits and forget that he'd said he was in love with her.

But it was difficult.

Especially when he looked so good, so familiar and so damned sexy.

"Ash," he beckoned softly. "Come here."

She remained where she was, her feet feeling as though they were encased in cement. Walking toward him would be a mistake. Being close to him in any way whatsoever would only weaken her resolve and commitment to end things before they really got started.

"I can't," she whispered.

"Sure you can," he said softly and held out his hand.

And then she moved. Without resistance, despite some

faraway voice telling her that it was crazy to go near him and risk her heart. But the pull that was uniquely his wrapped her up like a cocoon and seconds later she was in front of him, taking his hand. His fingers were warm as they enclosed around hers and Ash swayed toward him almost involuntarily.

"I wish..." Her words trailed and she took a breath. "I promised myself I wouldn't do this."

He tugged on her hand and she was quickly pressed against him. "I know. But we can't avoid the inevitable."

"We can. *I* can. I need to stop wanting you," she said, aching inside, because being so close to him was like heaven and hell at the same time. "The kids...the fact you're leaving in a few days...it's too hard..."

"Ash." He said her name so softly it was like a caress. "Some things are simply meant to be."

And then he kissed her. Softly. Deeply. Intimately. Each slant of his mouth against hers a seductive caress. Ash's hands moved to his chest and then curled around his shoulders, bringing them closer together. In the days since they'd last kissed she'd been dying inside, needing him like she needed air in her lungs, wanting him like she'd never wanted anyone before. And knowing it was mutual, knowing that Cole was as hungry for her as she was for him, only amplified every ounce of longing that thrummed through her body and heart.

"I should have known!"

A young, pain-filled voice ripped them apart immediately. *Maisy.* Ash stepped back guiltily. The girl looked furious. And rightly so. She longed to say something, but knew Cole had to handle the situation. She looked at him, saw his intense expression and remained silent.

"Maisy, honey, let me explain what—"

"I've got eyes," his daughter said, cutting him off and

breathing hard, her mouth pressed into a tight line. "And if you two have been screwing around I hope you remembered to use a rubber, *Cole*," she said crudely. "Because I bet the last thing you want is another visit from social services saying you've got another unwanted kid!"

Then she fled. Out of the barn and back to the cabin. Ash heard the cabin door slam and then turned toward Cole. "I'm so sorry. This shouldn't have happened. I knew it would end like this."

He let out a long and weary breath. "It's not your fault. I'll go and talk to her in a little while, and maybe give her some time to calm down."

"Maybe you should forget the space. She needs you, probably right now more than ever before. Being alone is the last thing she needs at this point."

He half shrugged. "I don't know what the hell to do," he said raggedly and then looked sheepish when he realized how much rage there was in his words. "Sorry… I'll talk to you later."

He walked from the barn and once he was twenty feet ahead she headed for the house. The kids were in the living room with Uncle Ted and she waved at them from the doorway, then made her way upstairs to shower and change before she started dinner. Half an hour later she was back downstairs and flouring chicken pieces for a casserole. Once dinner was in the pot she made peppermint tea and sat at the table, deep in thought.

"Are you okay, Mom?"

She looked up and spotted Jaye in the doorway. "Just fine, sweetie."

"You look sad," he said and ambled into the room. "Are you sad because Cole and Maisy are leaving soon?" He shrugged his bony shoulders. "'Cuz I know I am."

Ash knew the conversation was inevitable. Jaye adored

Cole and would miss him terribly. She offered a gentle smile. "We've talked about this before. You know that sometimes people come here just for a short time, because they need a certain kind of help. And Cole and Maisy—"

"It's different with them," Jaye said quietly. "Cole likes us. He likes Uncle Ted and Grandma and he likes me. And I know he likes you. A lot."

"I like him, too," she admitted and saw a gleam in her son's eyes. "But that doesn't change the reason they came here. And we must respect that and not make things more difficult by telling them we don't want them to leave, okay?"

His lips pressed together. "Even if it makes us sad?"

"Even then," she said, her throat suddenly burning with emotion.

"Maisy's lucky. I wish…" Jaye's voice trailed off and she watched him swallow hard. "I wish I had a dad like Cole."

Ash's pain was instantly amplified. She wanted to hold her son close and tell him that everything would return to normal soon. She wanted to tell him that they would be fine, as they had always been. But she couldn't. It would taste like a lie. Because she wasn't sure that anything would feel right ever again once Cole and Maisy left the ranch. "I tell you what, why don't you go up to their cabin and ask if they want to have dinner with us tonight, around six thirty. And if it's okay with Cole, you can spend some time with them before dinner."

Jaye's expression perked up. "Thanks, Mom."

He left and Ash busied herself with baking a pie for the next half hour. She was just whipping cream for topping when Cole emerged through the back door, tapping on the doorjamb before he entered.

"Hi," she said and placed the bowl on the countertop. "Everything okay?"

He shrugged wearily. "I thought I'd try and talk to my daughter now, is she in the living room?"

Ash stilled. "Isn't she in the cabin?"

Cole shook his head. "No. She wouldn't talk to me after...you know, what happened in the barn. I was in the shower when I heard the cabin door slam, I assumed she was here."

"She's not here." Ash came around the counter. "Where's Jaye? I sent him up to the cabin about half an hour ago, to invite you and Maisy for dinner."

Cole stepped closer. "Ash, the cabin is empty." He shook his head. "I haven't seen Jaye since earlier this afternoon."

Uneasiness crept up her spine. "Maybe they're in the barn. Or out by the stables."

But they weren't in the barn or stables. Or in the living room with Uncle Ted and Micah and Tahlia. And after a quick scour of the rest of the house, she followed Cole back to the cabin and they headed straight for Maisy's room, and quickly realized that her bag was missing.

"Don't panic," she advised him when they were back on the small porch, even though her heart was racing at a galloping speed. "I'm sure there is a logical explanation."

"Ash?"

She waved an arm in an arc. "She's probably gone off in a huff and Jaye has followed and—"

"Ash?" he said again, firmer this time.

"What?"

He moved closer. "The truck's gone."

Ash gasped and moved to look out the window. Sure enough, the undriven, untried truck that Cole had given to her days earlier was no longer in its spot beside the barn.

"Oh, God," she said and clutched at her throat. "You don't think…"

He nodded slowly. "I think we both know Maisy took the truck."

Her heart rammed behind her ribs. "Jaye…"

"And I think we both know that Jaye is probably with her."

Ash's insides turned to Jell-O as fear coursed through her blood. Because she knew he was right. There was no truck and no Maisy or Jaye. It was logical to assume the worst.

"I need to call the station and get a bulletin out ASAP."

But it was too little, too late. Because twenty minutes later she received a call from Hank Culhane saying that her son and Maisy had been involved in a single-vehicle accident on the outskirts of town and were on their way to the Cedar River Community Hospital, injured, but alive.

Cole drove her into town and the trip was done in an agonizing silence. She couldn't talk. Couldn't think. Couldn't do anything but wonder about the fate of her child. They reached the hospital in record time and Ash was thankful to see her friend Lucy attending in the ER. Even though Lucy was pregnant with her first child, she still worked part-time at the hospital. Much to Ash's relief. If her son was hurt she wanted her trusted friend attending to his injuries.

"He's okay," Lucy assured her, clearly taking in her pallor and the fear in Ash's eyes. "They're both okay. Jaye has a fractured arm, which will need to be set and put in a cast," she said and Ash's legs almost gave way. "And your daughter has a few cuts and bruises," Lucy said once Ash introduced him. "Actually, they were both very lucky. Hank said they skidded down an embankment and took out a fence."

"Can I see my son?" Ash tried to gain control of her breathing. Knowing Jaye was safe helped, but she'd been so frightened...

Lucy nodded and squeezed her arm. "Of course. They're both in triage. Come this way."

Ash could barely contain her emotion when she saw Jaye lying, eyes closed, on the bed, his left arm propped up on pillows and already turning a nasty shade of purple. She didn't look at Cole as he strode past her and down toward the far end of triage. She pulled up a chair and smoothed out her son's hair, and he opened his eyes.

"Hey, Mom," he said croakily.

"Hi, sweetie. I'm here."

He smiled and his eyes filled with tears. "Sorry about the truck."

"Don't worry about that," she assured him. "I only care that you're okay."

He winced. "I couldn't let her go alone, Mom. You understand, right?"

Ash swallowed hard and pressed her palm to her son's forehead. "I know, sweetie. I know."

She said a silent prayer, thanking the powers above for protecting her son, and then felt the tears on her cheeks. And she realized one heartbreaking fact. The sooner Cole Quartermaine was out of her life, the better.

Cole heard Maisy arguing with a nurse ten feet before he reached the triage cubicle.

"I said I was fine," his daughter complained. "I don't need to lie down. I don't need anything. My father will be here soon, so just stop poking at me and leave me alone."

He almost stopped in his tracks. *My father.* Just like that. Public recognition. Real and earnest acknowledgment. There wasn't sarcasm or cynicism in her words.

He'd been striding through triage imagining the worst, thinking she hated him and that he'd lost her to her anger and disappointment.

"Maisy?" he said, and stood by the curtain.

She looked up and her face crumpled as her shoulders sagged. "I'm...sorry."

The nurse offered him a comforting smile and nodded, leaving them alone. Cole sat beside her on the bed. She had a bruise on her temple and a narrow bandage on her forearm. But she was safe and alive and the knowledge filled him with relief. "What were you thinking?"

She shrugged hopelessly. "I wasn't. I just had to get away." She bit down on her bottom lip. "I guess I'm grounded now?"

"Is there any point?" he said and sighed wearily. "You know, I didn't teach you to drive so that you could end up here, Maisy."

"I know."

"And Jaye?"

She shrugged again and winced slightly. "He followed me. I said I was bailing and he got in the truck. The kid's persistent."

"You both could have been killed, do you realize that?"

"Yeah...I know," she said, getting visibly choked up. "But I wasn't driving fast, I promise. I just lost control and the truck bounced and then before I knew what was happening we had hit a fence."

"I was so worried about you."

Maisy met his gaze and looked at him, then inhaled a shuddering sigh and, somehow, she sagged against him. Cole wrapped his arm around her shoulders and she pressed her face into his shoulder, clearly all out of resistance.

"I'm sorry," she said, forcing out the words, and suddenly she clung to him. "I didn't mean to scare anyone. I know I do stupid things, but sometimes I can't help it." She gripped tighter. "Are you going to send me away? Are you going to send me back?"

"Send you back?"

"To social services," she said and hiccuped, her voice muffled against his shoulder.

Cole crumbled inside. "Of course not." He had his child in his arms and she was terrified he was going to send her away. "Maisy, I'm not going to send you away or leave you. Ever. I promise."

"Mom promised, too," she said, crying now. "She promised and then she left me alone."

Cole's heart felt as though it was being strangled. Her pain, her fear, became part of him and he pulled her close. "Honey, your mom got sick. She didn't leave you on purpose, or because of something you did. And you're not alone," he said gently, her quiet sobs tearing him up inside. "I'm here—I'll always be here. I'm your father, and you're a part of me."

"Why didn't Mom tell you about me?" she asked in an anguished voice.

Cole took a long breath. "I don't honestly know. But don't be mad at her, honey. She loved you and cared for you and although I can't promise not to die, I do promise that I'll always do everything I can to protect you and keep you safe."

"Promise?"

He smoothed back her hair from her face. "I promise," he assured her gently. "Maisy, I know you were angry about what you saw this afternoon. And I—"

"I'm not really angry," she said and hiccuped again. "I was just...surprised. And I freaked out. You know how I am sometimes. But I like Ash. She's really cool. And I get why you like her. Although, no one ever really wants to see their dad making out…it's kinda gross. Just like if you saw Pops and Nan, you know, doing…whatever."

Cole chuckled. *Dad. Pops. Nan.* It was as though someone had waved a magical wand and Maisy had somehow come to accept his family as her own. A deep and enduring love for his child washed over him and he knew in his heart that it was Ash who'd made the magic. Ash, with her gentle voice and caring arms. She'd wrapped Maisy in a secure embrace the moment they'd stepped onto the ranch. And his daughter had flourished beneath Ash's kindness and understanding.

"Okay, I hear what you're saying."

She smiled tentatively. "Um, is Jaye going to be all right?"

"The doctor said he has a fractured arm," Cole said quietly. "And will be in a cast for a while."

Maisy grimaced. "Ash must be so mad with me."

"She'll understand," he said, remaining positive for his daughter's sake. "How about you stay here for a while and I'll go and see how he's doing?"

She nodded. "You'll come back soon?"

Cole squeezed her shoulder. "Be right back. Get some rest."

He got to his feet and once she was settled back and resting, Cole pulled the curtain around and then headed toward the front of triage. Jaye was lying on a bed, his arm propped up on a pillow.

"Hey, Cole. I got a broken arm."

"So I heard," he said and smiled. "Where's your mom?"

"Talking to the police," he replied and waved his good arm. "Out there. You don't think me and Maisy will go to jail, do you?"

"No, kid. You'll be staying right here. But I need to talk to your mom for a minute, okay?"

Cole left the triage area and headed back out to reception. He spotted Ash talking with two uniformed officers and walked toward the group.

"They'll need a statement from Maisy," Ash said quietly when he approached. "Once the investigation is done you can get the truck towed."

Cole nodded, then answered a few questions and then provided his contact details. Once Maisy had given a statement, they spoke briefly to Jaye, who confirmed his daughter's story of the truck skidding and losing control. As the boy relayed the information he could feel Ash's anguish. Her arms were crossed, her jaw was tight and he knew she was barely holding on to her emotions. When Jaye was taken for an X-ray he remained with Maisy while Ash headed off to be with her son. Cole spoke to the doctor about his daughter and once a concussion was ruled out, he was told he would be able to take her home within the next couple of hours.

When she dozed off, Cole left the triage and went looking for Ash. He found her outside Radiology, sitting in a chair, hands in her lap. There was no one else around other than a receptionist behind a small reception desk and he wordlessly pulled up a chair and sat opposite Ash.

She looked up and met his gaze. "How's Maisy?"

"Fine," he replied. "No concussion, thank goodness. Just a few cuts and bruises. Ash, I know—"

"He wanted to help her," she said, her voice so tight it pained him. "Jaye said Maisy was upset and he didn't want her to be alone. She didn't know where she was going. What she was doing. Only that she wanted to run, to get away from you, from me…from the whole world."

"She's calmed down now. And she's okay. But she's concerned that you're angry with her."

Her shoulders twitched. "I'm not angry with Maisy. She's a child." She jumped to her feet and propped her hands on her hips. "Where were you?"

"What?"

"She packed her bag and stole the truck. Where were you when that was going on?"

Realization seeped through his blood. She wasn't angry with Maisy. She was angry with *him*. Cole slowly got to his feet. "When Maisy got back to the cabin she wouldn't talk to me. She was in her room with the door locked. I took a shower and when I got out she was gone. I thought she was up at the main house."

"But she wasn't," Ash said flatly. "I told you that she needed you. She saw us together and that triggered something inside her—emotion, fear, betrayal—and you needed to be there for the fallout. If you want to be a parent you don't get to do it when you feel like it. It's a full-time job, Cole."

Resentment quickly wound up his spine. "I know that. And I wasn't ignoring her, I tried to—"

"Trying's not good enough," she responded harshly. "You're her father, you don't try—you just *do*. But you were distracted, right? Caught up in this *thing* between us. Maybe wasting time thinking about how you'd get me into bed one more time before you leave? And while you were doing that, the safety of my son, *my child*, was put at risk."

It was quite the accusation, and Cole's immediate thought was to mount a counteroffensive and demand why she'd let her son out of her sight. But she looked exhausted and overwrought and the last thing he wanted to do was magnify her distress. Plus, there was an element of truth in her words that needled at him. He *had* been distracted.

Maisy's outburst in the barn had torn him in two. Because he knew he needed to be there for his daughter, but he also knew that the knowledge he was leaving the ranch in a matter of days was beating him up inside. And instead of insisting Maisy talk to him about her feelings, he'd taken the easy route and given her the space she craved, knowing it was exactly the opposite of what he should have done.

He inhaled deeply. "You're upset and concerned about Jaye. I get that. So how about we—"

"Don't you dare patronize me, Cole," she stormed. "I'm over being wrapped up in your good looks and charm. I'm...*done*. Whatever we had, it's over." She turned and took a few steps away from him, her entire body heaving. When she turned back there were tears in her eyes and rage in her expression. "I wish you'd never come here."

Her words hurt, deep down, like they were obviously meant to. He couldn't speak, couldn't say anything to ease her pain and anger. She was done. It was over. He nodded, aching right down through to his soul, and then slowly walked away.

Chapter Twelve

Saying goodbye was never easy. Ash had done it countless times over the years. Children came and then went. Families were reunited. But saying goodbye to Maisy and Cole was one of the hardest things Ash had ever done. It didn't help that Nancy had tears in her eyes, or that Uncle Ted was no better and Jaye was trying valiantly to stand stoic and strong beside her, while Tahlia and Micah clung onto her hands. It also didn't help that she and Cole had barely exchanged words since the night at the hospital. Maisy was still sporting a few bruises and Jaye had a bright yellow cast on his arm, but the real wounds ran much deeper.

Watching him load the bags into the rental car, witnessing Maisy's obvious unhappiness that she was leaving the ranch, made Ash ache all over. The kids all hugged her, and watching Jaye and Maisy hold on to one another made her throat burn with a kind of raw emotion she could hardly compartmentalize. But it was when Jaye hugged

Cole that she experienced the real, bone-wrenching reality of the situation.

"You take care, buddy," Cole said and hugged him tightly. "Look after your mom."

"I will," Jaye promised. "I'm gonna miss you."

"Me, too," Cole said and released him and then looked toward Ash. "Thank you for everything."

He held out his hand and she took it tentatively, her knees almost giving way as their skin connected. Electricity shot up her arm as his grip tightened. Ash let out a shallow breath. She didn't want to touch him. She didn't want to remember or yearn or feel anything. "Good luck," she said and then quickly withdrew her hand. "Goodbye."

And within minutes the car was driving off, dust in its wake.

After they left the mood around the ranch was somber. Uncle Ted did his best to amuse the kids with a video game and after an hour of trying to do some paperwork, Ash headed for the kitchen to make tea. She was dipping a tea bag into a stone mug when Nicola appeared in the doorway.

"Your mom called," her friend said and smiled. "She said you might need someone to talk to."

Ash beckoned her into the room and took out another mug. "My mother is a smart woman."

"Yes," Nancy said from behind Nicola. "I am. I'll have some of that tea if you're making it."

A few minutes later she was sitting at the kitchen table, her chin in her hands. Looking across at her mother and friend. "So, is this meant to be an intervention?"

"No," her mother said. "But I am concerned about you."

"I'm fine, Mom. Never better."

"You know, it's okay to be upset that he's gone."

"He?" Ash shook her head. "Mom, you're the world's

worst matchmaker. And if you must know, I'm glad he's not here anymore. Things can get back to normal."

Nancy's dramatic brows rose. "Normal. You mean dull. That young man brought this place to life. He brought *you* to life."

She knew her mother didn't mean to hurt her, but she was hurt. "I liked my life the way it was before Cole crashed into it. I felt safe and content."

"Scared and lonely," Nancy said. "You know, it's okay to admit that you fell for him."

"I didn't," she argued. "That would be stupid. He came here to work on his relationship with his daughter. I'm not going to waste time imagining his time here was anything more than that. Or that it *could* be anything more than that. He's gone. End of story."

Gone.

He left.

Men always leave me.

Ash didn't allow the words to leave her tongue. She didn't want pity or commiseration. Cole had been gone barely a few hours and she already missed him. She missed his smile, his deep voice, his loping gait. His kiss. His touch. And she ached knowing she would never see him again. But she was right to end things. Life had to return to normal. And it would.

"It's good that he patched things up with his daughter," Nicola said and drank some tea.

Ash nodded. "I really do think they'll work it out."

"Things often have a way of doing that," her friend said. "Look at how things worked out for Kayla and Liam. And Brooke and Tyler. See, love really does conquer all."

Ash managed a laugh. "Since when did you become so sentimental? Or have you been hanging around my mother?"

Nicola shrugged. "Maybe it's when I saw you and Cole together."

Ash's insides constricted. Nicola was being fanciful and overly romantic and she wasn't going to get drawn into the conversation any deeper. Cole was gone and she would never see him again. End of story.

"I want to forget about him," she said and took a long breath. "I *have* to."

And as the days blended into one another and a week passed, Ash got back into the rhythm of her life. Sort of. She went to work, spent time with the kids and met Nicola for coffee, ignoring every attempt her friend made to bring up Cole's name in the conversation.

"Have you heard from him?" Nicola asked on a Friday afternoon when they met for coffee and cake at the Muffin Box café.

"No," she replied. "And I don't expect to. I think Maisy and Jaye have texted a few times. And I spoke to Ricky, who's been texting Maisy, and apparently she's back at school and doing okay."

"I thought Cole might have called you."

"I made it pretty clear I wanted to end things."

"Because you blame him for the accident?"

She'd talked to Nicola about it, and said aloud it sounded irrational. But she couldn't help how she felt. If she and Cole hadn't been acting like a pair of lustful teenagers, then Maisy would never have caught them in the barn and the accident would never have happened. So, even if her anger was misdirected, she couldn't help herself. She needed to blame Cole to keep him at a distance and somehow work out how to forget all about him and the weeks they had spent together.

Which might have been easier had he not continued to invade her life. Because when she arrived home that afternoon there was a bright red pickup in her driveway, bigger and more robust than the silver one Maisy had crashed down the embankment. That one had ended up at the wrecking yard behind Joss Culhane's garage and she'd made it abundantly clear that she wanted nothing to do with the vehicle. This one was bigger and looked even more expensive. And she knew immediately that the new truck was from Cole. Uncle Ted was standing by the steps and he smiled as she got out of her battered old truck and then stared long and hard at the shiny pickup.

"This is for you," her uncle said and passed her an envelope.

There was a card inside, with a note written in a dark, masculine scrawl.

Ash, I know you probably have steam coming out of your ears right about now. But, just keep steaming and take this in the spirit with which it's given. You need a new truck and we both know you're too stubborn to admit it. So, take this as a gesture of my gratitude for all you have done for my daughter. And please know that despite how badly things ended between us, I don't regret one moment of the time we had together.

Cole.

Ash was still looking at the note days later. It was crumpled and dog-eared and had been refolded a dozen times. But she still didn't drive the truck, even though she was sorely tempted. It seemed wrong and she didn't want to be drawn further into his web. It had to go back. She called Joss and he only laughed at her and said Cole had made it very clear she was to keep the vehicle. Of course, Jaye and everyone else looked at her as though she was a crazy person. But she wasn't going to be swayed. She was going to stick to her principles. She didn't want his stupid truck. She just wanted him out of her head and out of her life.

Which, she discovered the following Wednesday afternoon, was becoming impossible. Because at four thirty that afternoon, a cab pulled up in the driveway and a passenger got out, dragging a small tote. A girl with dark hair and blue eyes.

Maisy was back!

Cole was glad to be back in Arizona. Five days of hotels, meetings and airline food was more than enough. Despite his mood, it had been a successful trip. He'd signed on a substantial new sponsor for the team and ensured Quartermaine Racing would be on the circuit for the next five seasons. In another time, another life, he would have been doing backflips about such a deal. But all he felt was numb through to his bones. And lonelier than he'd imagined possible.

Which was stupid and foolhardy. He had his life back. His family. His apartment. His work and his friends. Everything was as it had been before he'd gone to Cedar River. Only better, because now he had a real relationship with his daughter. Maisy talked to him. She laughed around him. She didn't scowl and hide in her room the moment she got home from school.

He should have been jumping through hoops, shouting off rooftops, singing in the rain...but all he had inside was the energy to simply get up every day and breath in and out and forget that he'd been shown a glimpse of a life he would never have.

A life he wanted.

And a love he needed.

But there was no hope, no chance of making it work. Ash had made her feelings abundantly clear.

I wish you'd never come here...

The anguish in her voice had spoken volumes. And the regret had been written all over her beautiful face. They were too different and the thousand miles between their lives was as difficult as if they'd lived on separate planets. There was no middle road. Her life. His life. And no life in between.

Now, he had to work out a way to be happy and content with his real life. He had to stop closing down every time he was around his family. He had to learn to get satisfaction from his career. He had to open his mind up to the possibility of dating. He had to join in and become a part of his own life.

Easy.

Right.

Not when he felt like his heart had been smashed into the dust.

Cole had been back in Phoenix for precisely forty-five minutes when he realized something was not quite right. He called his sister Scarlett from the airport and said he'd swing by her apartment to pick up Maisy. Scarlett informed him that Maisy had said she was staying at their parents' house while he was away.

He called Maisy's cell and left a message when she didn't pick up, then got his car from the long-term parking area and drove directly to his folks' house in Encanto. It took five minutes to work out that Maisy was not staying with his parents. He couldn't understand it. Things had been better. Good. They were getting along, becoming a family. It didn't make sense. He was just about to head back to his apartment and start calling some of her friends before he rang the police, when his cell buzzed.

He checked the screen, hoping it was his daughter, but it was a number he didn't immediately recognize.

"Cole, it's Ash."

Her voice warmed his blood with a longing so intense he could barely breathe. But he had to concentrate on finding Maisy. "Ash, I can't talk right—"

"She's here, Cole," Ash said quietly. "Maisy arrived here about half an hour ago."

His daughter was in South Dakota? "How the hell did she get there?"

"Bus, I think. Anyway, she's safe and she's okay."

"She was supposed to be staying with my sister," he explained, hating that she'd think him even more of an irresponsible parent than usual. "I've been on the road for a few days, with meetings in Dallas and several other cities." He breathed a heavy sigh of relief. "Are you sure she's okay?"

"Positive."

"I'll be there as soon as I can," he assured her. "And Ash…thanks."

She ended the call and then Cole turned toward his startled parents. "She's in South Dakota."

"Why?" his mother asked.

Cole shrugged. "I don't know. Things have been good… better. She's settled at school and we've been working things out. She's even talked about her mom." He shook his head. "I don't know why she ran away. All I know is that I need to go and get her."

His mother nodded. "Yes, and we're coming with you."

Cole stared at his parents. "Mom, I don't think—"

"Maisy needs to see that we all care about her. She's our granddaughter, as much a part of us as she is a part of you." Zara smiled gently. "And you have some unfinished business up there. We can all see how unhappy you are, Cole. Your father and I are not blind. *We know.*"

"You know?"

"We know that you've got it bad for Ash McCune," his father said bluntly. "We know that Phoenix is the last place you want to be right now. And we know that you *don't know* what to do about it. Well, here's the thing, son—you won't know stuck down here being torn up inside."

Cole ignored the compression in his chest. "She doesn't want me," he said and ached all over once the words left his mouth.

"You sure about that?" his father asked and grinned.

Cole ran a frustrated hand through his hair. "Even if she did, her life is there. Mine is here."

"Your life," his father said and wrapped an arm around his mom's waist, "is wherever you are *present*. So, go and be present. Be with your family. What have you got to lose?"

Pride. Dignity. My soul. My heart.

"Everything."

But then he looked at his parents, happy and in love after nearly forty years together, and still as much in love now as they were when they first met. Despite all the challenges they'd been through. They were together. A tight unit. Husband and wife. Bound to one another by love and respect and loyalty. All the things he believed a relationship should be. And he knew that his disastrous marriage to Valerie had soured him and since the divorce he'd refused to lay his heart on the line, determined to never feel so raw and vulnerable again. Until he'd met Ash. His fear and reticence had disappeared the moment he'd kissed her. Her goodness and kindness, her soft words and tender touch, were like a homing beacon. Maisy knew that. Maisy had more sense than he did.

His beautiful and vibrant and challenging daughter had gone home.

It was time he did, too.

In the twenty-four hours since Maisy had been on the ranch, Ash was no closer to understanding why the teenager had run away. Things were good at home. She was getting along much better with her father. The very fact she referred to Cole as *her father* indicated that she'd settled into their relationship and was willing to be his daughter.

Still, Ash couldn't quell the uneasiness inside her heart. Something was obviously wrong. All Maisy would say was that she missed the ranch and Jaye and Uncle Ted and everyone else and wanted to come back for a visit. And it was her mother who eventually verbalized what Ash secretly suspected.

"The girl is matchmaking."

She was on the porch with Nancy, sitting in the love seat. "What?"

"Doing what I failed to do," her mother said and grinned. "Well, he's on his way back here, isn't he?"

Ash nodded. She'd received a text message from Cole saying he'd arrived in Rapid City and would be at the ranch within the hour. And her nerves were shot. He was coming back. She would have to see him again. Talk to him. It was hard enough hearing his voice over the phone—the thought of seeing him, of having him within touching distance, was almost too much to bear.

"He's coming to collect his daughter, that's all."

"Yes, dear, of course he is," Nancy said and grinned as a sleek gray car turned into the driveway.

Ash got to her feet and stood by the railing and waited as the vehicle headed for the house. The front screen opened and Maisy emerged, with Jaye and Micah and Tahlia close behind him. The car pulled up in the driveway and Cole got out. He looked achingly familiar and so handsome, dressed in dark trousers and a blue shirt that stretched across his broad shoulders. Two other people emerged from the car and she quickly recognized his parents.

"Dad!" Maisy squealed and then raced down the stairs and headed straight for him.

Ash's heart almost burst through her chest when she witnessed his reaction as Maisy joyfully announced that he was her father. Within seconds the teenager was in his arms, hugging him close. And then every fear, every ounce of reluctance she'd harbored over the past twenty-four hours knowing she would see him again, suddenly vanished. This moment is what she'd longed for since the day they had first arrived so many weeks earlier.

She watched, mesmerized as they spoke for a moment, and then once Maisy had hugged her grandparents, the girl pointed toward the house. Ash stilled, unable to move, her legs like lead as he kissed Maisy's forehead and then walked toward the steps. Once he reached the bottom rung, he spoke.

"Hi."

Ash nodded, emotion clutching her throat. "She called you Dad."

"I know," he said, his voice low and husky and like a seductive caress across her skin. "It feels good."

"And you bought me another truck?"

He half shrugged. "It's a gift."

"Extravagant," she said, trying to keep her wits. "And too much."

"I have my daughter because of you," he said quietly. "So, nothing seems adequate."

Her heart rolled over. "You've worked hard to get to this point."

"Have I?" He shrugged and shook his head. "I'm not so sure. You were right. That night at the hospital, you were right to say what you did. I *was* distracted. I was thinking about a hundred other things when I should have been focused on my daughter. But I have to accept that I'm not going to get this fatherhood thing right every time. I'm going to screw up and make mistakes and get through it the best I can. I guess that's what being a parent is—doing your best."

Ash let out a long breath. He was so right. Parenting wasn't an exact science. Everyone made mistakes. She did. "Maisy looks happy, so you're doing okay. I'm glad it's all worked out."

He rocked back a little on his heels. "Well, actually, it hasn't *all* worked out." His gaze was blisteringly intense, capturing hers effortlessly. There was heat and awareness and something else, something she didn't want to acknowledge. "But, I'm hopeful that it might."

Ash's entire body stilled. "What—what does that mean?"

He smiled. And how she longed for his smile. It was captivating, shattering her into a thousand tiny pieces. He put one hand up and then suddenly focused his attention onto Jaye. "Hey, buddy, how are you doing?"

Jaye beamed at him. "I'm good. My cast comes off in three weeks," he said proudly.

Cole smiled again. "So, Jaye, here's the thing… I'd like your permission to ask your mom to marry me."

There was a kind of insane, screeching silence for a moment. She could feel her mother's shock, could see Maisy's excitement and his parents' obvious approval. And Jaye looked as though he was about to jump clean out of his own skin. And Ash couldn't speak. Couldn't think. Couldn't allow herself to believe she'd heard him correctly. Until she finally found her voice.

"What are you doing?"

But he didn't respond. He was still looking at her son and waiting for his response.

Then Jaye spoke. "Does that mean you'll be my dad, like my dad for real? And like…forever?"

Cole nodded. "Absolutely."

Jaye pumped a fist in the air. "Yes!" He turned toward Ash. "Say yes, Mom. Make sure you say yes."

Ash could barely breathe and finally drew in a shuddering sigh. "Are you out of your mind?"

Cole laughed. "Probably," he said and put a hand to his chest. "But I love you. And I don't want to waste another minute of my life thinking about all the reasons why this couldn't possibly work out."

I love you…

The words were out, for everyone to hear. And no one seemed as shocked as she was.

But she had to keep her head and her good sense. "How about the fact that I live here and you live in Arizona?"

"I'll live wherever you are. I want to be here," he said and waved a loose arm. "I want to do something valuable here, with you. I haven't been truly content for a long time," he admitted. "When I stopped racing I gave up a big part of who I was. And I've been struggling to find myself again. And I have. Right here. On this ranch. I've discovered that I love being a father, but I want to share that with you. I want to do all this," he said and waved his arm around. "*With you.* I want my child to be yours. I want your child to be mine. And I want us to make babies together—I want us to make Maisy and Jaye all over again." He sucked in a long, almost painful-sounding breath. "And I know you're terrified," he said gently. "I know every man who should have been there for you has left. And I know you think I'll probably do the same. But

I won't," he assured her. "You have my heart and soul, Ash. All of me. Everything I am. Forever."

Her heart surged with a sudden yearning to believe him, to believe she could have the fairy tale. Once, long ago, she'd believed in them. She'd longed for a happily-ever-after. And then through loss and disappointment, she'd become cynical and closed off. And afraid. As soon as he'd scraped the surface of her insecurities she'd pushed him away. And she lied, to him and herself. She didn't wish he'd never come to Cedar River. Because trying to imagine her life without Cole in it suddenly seemed like the worst kind of hell.

"I want to believe you, but—"

"Believe him, Mom," Jaye implored and urged her forward. "You know Cole's the best."

She did know. As did her son. Before she'd been able to see what a kind, compassionate and honorable man he was, her son had known. Her beautiful son had clung to Cole from the first, sensing that he was exactly what he needed in his young life. What they all needed, she'd discovered. Because she *did* need him. Like air in her lungs and like ground beneath her feet.

And suddenly, it all seemed so simple. So right. She took a deep breath and spoke what was singing in her heart.

"I love you, too."

And then pandemonium broke out. Jaye did his fist-pumping thing over and over, Maisy was dancing around her grandparents, her mother was hugging Uncle Ted, and Micah and Tahlia were racing around the porch in circles. Even the dogs seemed overjoyed as they raced around the yard. The goats were bleating and Rodney was chasing the chickens.

And while this was going on, Cole remained where he

was at the bottom of the steps, holding her gaze within his in a way that spoke volumes.

"Will you marry me?" he asked simply, beautifully and romantically.

Ash's entire body hummed and suddenly she heard only him, despite the joyful chaos now going on around them. And she nodded, smiling, her heart so filled with love she could barely keep it in her chest. "Yes."

He was up the steps in two seconds flat and then she was in his arms, exactly where she wanted to be. And he kissed her, cradling her neck, anchoring her head in that gentle way she'd become so accustomed to.

When he lifted his head, Ash was breathless and laughing and so incandescently happy she could barely stand. But it didn't matter, because he had her. He held her up. Gave her strength. Made her whole.

He pulled back and withdrew a small box from his pocket. Ash took the box with tentative fingers and pried open the lid. Inside a cushion of velvet sat a perfectly beautiful ring, emeralds and diamonds in a platinum band.

"It was my grandmother's," he explained as he took the ring and slipped it onto her finger. "She was a fiery redhead just like you."

Ash pushed up on her toes and kissed his mouth lingeringly. "It's perfect."

She looked down and saw her family and his all standing at the bottom of the steps, all beaming, all laughing and hugging one another in a way that families do. Her full heart brimmed over when she thought of all they had. She had a new daughter. He had a son. Their kids had more grandparents and aunts and uncles. And one day, perhaps they would be blessed with more children. She turned her face back toward Cole and saw that he was watching her with blistering intensity. And love. And he knew exactly what she was thinking.

"We made this," he said and urged her closer. "You and me. And it feels good."

"Better than good," she said and wrapped her arms around him. "The best. We make an amazing family."

And that, she thought as he kissed her again, was everything.

Epilogue

Four and a half months later...

Ash hadn't imagined anything would surpass the joy she'd felt on her wedding day barely four months earlier. But it did. This did. The papers were all signed. The correct processes had been followed. As of eleven o'clock that morning, Micah and Tahlia were officially their son and daughter.

It had been Cole's idea to legally adopt them and Ash had only needed a microsecond to agree. Since they had been in her care for nearly a year, their case worker had pushed the paperwork through as quickly as possible. And now it was official, and JoJo's was the perfect place to celebrate. Everyone was here and Nicola had booked the entire restaurant for them so they could enjoy the event with their friends and family.

The last six months had been a whirlwind of the best

kind. She'd fallen in love, married and now was mother to four incredible kids.

Ash touched her belly lovingly. She was barely two months along in her pregnancy and had only made the discovery that morning after taking a hurriedly purchased pregnancy test when she realized she was late with her period. With the excitement and anticipation surrounding the adoption, she'd kept the news to herself, waiting for the perfect moment to tell her husband and then the world.

And since the smell of pizza was making her queasy, Ash figured she'd have to tell him soon. Like, right now. Which was opportune because he had just finished making a speech about family and kids and the restaurant had erupted in laughter and congratulations.

"Everything okay?" Cole asked as people started milling around the dessert table and as he came behind her and placed his hands on her hips.

"Perfect," she said and swayed against him. "I'm so happy."

He rested his chin on the top of her head. "I know that feeling. The kids look happy, too."

Ash looked toward the booth seats and smiled. Maisy and Jaye were holding court. Micah and Tahlia were scarfing down slices of the cake baked in their honor. Brooke and Tyler were there with their toddler and Lucy stood beside her husband and newborn son. Kayla and Liam were sitting down, since Kayla was heavily pregnant and due within weeks. Nancy had brought along her new boyfriend, Rex, who worked as a foreman on one of the local ranches. He was a nice man and her mom seemed truly happy for the first time in forever. Uncle Ted was chatting with Nicola, and Cole's parents and sisters had arrived the day before to share in their celebrations. Several of her work colleagues had dropped by along with some other friends and Ash experienced happiness that was so acute she could barely breathe. It was as though she suddenly had this perfect life. Maisy and Jaye had both enrolled at the local high school. Jaye's transition from home-schooling to regular school had been an easy decision and her son was flourishing in his classes and had made some great friends. And her son adored Cole and for the first time had someone he could call Dad. Which he did, every chance he got. His eagerness to be Cole's son warmed her through to her bones and now that Micah and Tahlia's adoption was finalized, she knew Jaye was itching to be next. He'd made it very clear he wanted to be Jaye Quartermaine.

She turned in his arms. "I love you, Cole."

"I know," he said and grinned. "Do you know what else, I feel incredibly blessed. Six months ago I never would have imagined that I would be married with four kids."

Ash took a breath and rubbed his hand. "Five."

"Yeah, and I just couldn't…"

His words trailed off and he stared down into her up-turned face. "What?"

She grabbed his hand and moved it down, resting it discreetly against her belly. "Five." Cole couldn't breathe. Or swallow. Or move. His beautiful wife was staring up at him, her green eyes shining with pure joy and love. A love that humbled him through to his bones.

"You're pregnant?" he asked, whisper-soft.

She nodded and smiled. "Yes."

The idea that he had made a child with her, that a tiny human would come into the world who was a part of them both, filled him in a way he could barely fathom. So much had changed in his life. Merging their families together. Working out a way to remain a part of the racing business from South Dakota. It had been hard at first, but he'd made it work. He managed the race team's marketing and PR and although he commuted once a month to Phoenix, he always knew Cedar River would call him home. He loved living on the ranch. They had plans to build another two cottages and finish renovating the main house. Ash had accepted the promotion to sergeant and it had all, somehow, come to fit together like a perfect jigsaw puzzle.

And now, this last piece made them complete. A baby. Which would mean sleepless nights and diapers and everything else. And it was all he wanted.

"Yours, mine and ours," she said and cupped his cheek.

"Just *ours*," he said and pressed close. "For always."

Ash smiled lovingly. "I like the sound of that."

* * * * *

Don't miss Nicola and Kieran's story,
the next installment in Helen Lacey's series

THE CEDAR RIVER COWBOYS
Coming soon to Mills & Boon Cherish!

MILLS & BOON®

Cherish™

EXPERIENCE THE ULTIMATE RUSH OF FALLING IN LOVE

MILLS & BOON®

EXCLUSIVE EXTRACT

Artist Holly Motta arrives in New York to find billionaire Ethan Benton in the apartment where *she's* meant to be staying! And the next surprise? Ethan needs a fake fiancée and he wants *her* for the role…

Read on for a sneak preview of
HER NEW YORK BILLIONAIRE
by debut author Andrea Bolter

"In exchange for you posing as my fiancée, as I have outlined, you will be financially compensated and you will become legal owner of this apartment and any items such as clothes and jewels that have been purchased for this position. Your brother's career will not be impacted negatively should our work together come to an end. *And…*" He paused for emphasis.

Holly leaned forward in her chair, her back still board-straight.

"I have a five-building development under construction in Chelsea. There will be furnished apartments, office lofts and common space lobbies – all in need of artwork. I will commission you for the project."

Holly's lungs emptied. A commission for a big corporate project. That was exactly what she'd hoped she'd find in New York. A chance to have her work seen by thousands of people. The kind of exposure that could lead from one job to the next and to a sustained and successful career.

This was all too much. Fantastic, frightening, impossible… Obviously getting involved in any way with Ethan Benton was a terrible idea. She'd be beholden to him. Serving another person's agenda again. Just what she'd come to New York to get away from.

But this could be a once-in-a-lifetime opportunity. An apartment. A job. It sounded as if he was open to most any demand she could come up with. She really did owe it to herself to contemplate this opportunity.

Her brain was no longer operating normally. The clock on Ethan's desk reminded her that it was after midnight. She'd left Fort Pierce early that morning.

"That really is an incredible offer..." She exhaled. "But I'm too tired to think straight. I'm going to need to sleep on it."

"As you wish."

Holly moved to collect the luggage she'd arrived with. Ethan beat her to it and hoisted the duffle bag over his shoulder. He wrenched the handle of the suitcase. Its wheels tottered as fast as her mind whirled as she followed him to the bedroom.

"Goodnight, then." He placed the bags just inside the doorway and couldn't get out of the room fast enough.

Before closing the door she poked her head out and called, "Ethan Benton, you don't play fair."

Over his shoulder, he turned his face back toward her. "I told you. I always get what I want."

Don't miss
HER NEW YORK BILLIONAIRE
by exciting new author
Andrea Bolter

Available September 2017
www.millsandboon.co.uk

MILLS & BOON®

Why shop at millsandboon.co.uk?

Each year, thousands of romance readers
find their perfect read at millsandboon.co.uk.
That's because we're passionate about
bringing you the very best romantic fiction.
Here are some of the advantages of
shopping at www.millsandboon.co.uk:

* **Get new books first**—you'll be able to buy
  your favourite books one month before they
  hit the shops

* **Get exclusive discounts**—you'll also be
  able to buy our specially created monthly
  collections, with up to 50% off the RRP

* **Find your favourite authors**—latest news,
  interviews and new releases for all your
  favourite authors and series on our website,
  plus ideas for what to try next

* **Join in**—once you've bought your favourite
  books, don't forget to register with us to rate,
  review and join in the discussions

Visit **www.millsandboon.co.uk**
for all this and more today!